6. 4. 1f

Born in 1949, Sue was brought up by her grandmother and had an unusual childhood. On leaving school she studied Business studies and then later joined the police, where she served in many roles for twenty-eight years, retiring as a village police officer riding a motor cycle. On retiring, she went to agricultural college and then lived for some years on an isolated smallholding in the Yorkshire Dales, keeping rare breed sheep. She worked in many different jobs, including on the railway, as a kitchen porter, a housekeeper and as a chef. She has now retired and lives in comparative comfort in the Yorkshire Wolds, and writes a weekly diary in the Yorkshire Post.

Also by the same Author

The Cellar Pets

The Wyvern Rebellion

Murder at the Brass Cat

OPERATION CAIN

SHEPHERD'S MYSTERY

Sue Woodcock

OPERATION CAIN

SHEPHERD'S MYSTERY

Vanguard Press

A CIP catalogue record for this title is
available from the British Library.

ISBN 978 1 784651 92 3

*Vanguard Press is an imprint of
Pegasus Elliot MacKenzie Publishers Ltd.*
www.pegasuspublishers.com

First Published in 2016

**Vanguard Press
Sheraton House Castle Park
Cambridge England**

Printed & Bound in Great Britain by CMP (uk) Limited

This book is dedicated to my friends Mark and Julie, for their enthusiastic encouragement, and to my friend Jane Wynn, the best shepherd I have ever known.

The Book of Genesis

Chapter 4

V1   And Adam knew Eve his wife; and she conceived and bare Cain and said I have gotten a man from the LORD.

V2   And she again bare his brother Abel. And Abel was a keeper of sheep but Cain was a tiller of the ground.

V8   And Cain talked with Abel his brother; and it came to pass when they were in the field, that Cain rose up against his brother and slew him.

Dramatis Personae

The Train Journey
The Lucky Horse Shoe B&B

Train Driver	Neil
Tom and Eileen Roberts	
Signalman	Tommy
dog	Roy
Guard	John
Passengers	Donna
	Aiden

The Agricultural College

Principal	Professor Hardaker
Sheep Tutor	Michael John Grady (Tigger)
Wife	Susan
Step-daughter	Karen
Shepherd	Nick Greenwood
Farm Secretary	Rachel
Equine Staff	Collette
Equine Student	Zoe

Sheep Course

Steve (Irish)	Diana Green	dog, Drift
Alison (Canadian)	Eddie Sullivan	dog, Biff
Janet (Alias Charles Avington)		dog, Bet
Ruth	Amy	
Peter (Haggis)	Alex	
David Long		

The Police
Local Station

WPC 213 Sandra Lancashire
Sergeant Cole
Inspector Lorraine Bradley
Detective Chief Inspector Roger Thornaby
Detective Sergeant Bernie Rush
WPC Makin
DC Simon Alder
WPC Drey

Police Headquarters

Assistant Chief Constable	'O' Gaskell
Assistant Chief Constable	Kitchen

Others

Wally (Superintendent)   Wife – Gwen
Technical Services   Ivan – son Jeremy
Inspector Collingwood   Complaints and Discipline
Sergeant, 'Operations'   Callum Doyle – Firearms
                                                    user

Inspector, 'Operations'   Terry

National Security

Mr Smith
Mr Jones

City Station

Inspector Smith   PC Oxted   Jack

Murder Squad

Detective Chief Superintendent Saul Catchpole
                          wife – Anna
                          Sons – Sam, Stephen
                          Dogs – Hector, Lysander
Detective Inspector   Celia Allenby
Detective Sergeants   Geoff Bickerstaff, Paul
Detective Constables   Julie, Darren, Kate, Tarik,
                          David, Toby, Bert

Clerical Office Staff

Nita Patel
Fred Dunlop
Lauren Bakeup

Others
Farmers

Dominic Mc Gill, widow Gillian
Billy Birtwhistle
Jim Gardener
Farm manager – Donald
Water Board Maintenance man – Albert Gatsby

Chapter One

The old railway sidings were spooky at night. Neil always got the shivers when he made his way down the side of the tracks to collect the early engine. During the winter months the darkness was almost complete as you walked under the gantry towards the cab. Further down the track he could see the lights from the signal box, which made where he was seem even blacker. It was only his strong torch beam that kept him from tripping over the loose chippings and weeds in the cess beside the line. Although he had been walking to work on this route for several years, he always felt safer once he had made it to the cab.

As he passed under the signal gantry he once again felt a chill. His fellow drivers told stories of a ghostly figure that sometimes flitted across the railway lines, just at the edge of the torch beam. Neil had never seen it but the place was depressing. He looked up, just to check, as he always did but this time he was shocked when he saw a figure moving across the line ahead of him. He called out, "Who's there? Get off the line, you prat, the 3.17 down train is due any minute."

There was no reply and no sound at all. He knew better than to try to find them even though his torch had a strong beam and he hurried on to his cab, and once inside the engine breathed a sigh of relief. He checked the cab over and realized he was a few minutes early. He slipped back down from the engine and went to the signal phone by the line. The signalman answered immediately.

Neil was rather relieved and said, "Tommy, I thought I saw someone on the line just now, did you see anything?"

"No, Neil, I didn't, but I heard you shout. Are you all right?"

"Yes, I must be imagining things. Is the early up goods on time?"

"It's running three minutes late, but once it's through I will let you go. How is the wife?"

"Doing well, thanks."

"And the baby, I heard it was a boy, all well?"

"Yes, he is fine we are calling him Colin Richard."

"Good names. Have a good day, mate."

As Neil waited for the early train to pass through, he paused to reflect on what he had seen. On each occasion the 'ghost' had been seen, something unpleasant had befallen the person seeing it. Nothing fatal for them, but Arnie had seen it twice and each time he had hit a 'jumper' on the line. Then Imran had witnessed a fatal car crash on his way home from work. Wilf had had a passenger die of a heart attack after he had seen the ghost. Soon the goods lumbered past him and he needed to concentrate on what he was doing. He jotted down the sighting in the incident log in the cab, while he waited at the station for the early passengers to board.

It was his second trip of the day, and still early in the morning, when he remembered it again. It was light by this time and he slowed for the twenty-miles-per-hour restriction, and then had to stop for a red signal. He needed to get down from the engine, and ring in. A delay there was not unusual. He knew the area well. As he waited for the signalman to answer the phone, he looked down the embankment towards the agricultural college grounds. He often saw the early duty students either working the sheep, or exercising their dogs on the nearby field. Unusually there was no one around, but as he finished his call, he turned to climb back to his cab. He looked down to the bottom of the bank. In the ditch, almost hidden by the long grass and thistles was a person, a very still person. He rang the signalman back, and then clambered down the bank. His guard, John, joined him as he got to the bottom of the embankment, and they approached the still form lying in the ditch.

"Hell, Neil, is that what I think it is?"

"I hope it is a drunk, but I don't think so."

Together they got to the still form, and turned it over. It was a man, of about forty with short fair hair. That he was dead was very obvious. The massive wounds on his body had left a pool of sticky blood over the grass. John, a newly qualified and quite young guard, turned and rushed away and was violently sick a short distance away. Feeling somewhat nauseous himself Neil checked for a pulse, but found nothing. The body was stiff. He looked up at John who had gone a sort of green colour.

"Come on, lad, back to the train. We have a job to do. I will ring this in, I need you to reassure the passengers, who I hope have not seen this. I think we need to move the train on."

As John got back to the train, Neil was telling the signalman what he had found, and then waited until the signalman rang back with instructions. He looked around, and saw no one and although he heard a sort of squelching sound, could see nothing that caused it. There was a strange smell, one he could not identify. He could identify the smell of vomit, however. He too felt very queasy. The phone rang and he picked it up.

"Right, mate, move the train on to the next station. Another driver and guard will be there to take over from you. You are to wait there until the cops turn up. I have rung them and they are on their way. How many passengers have you?"

"About a dozen I think. I don't think they have seen it. Young John locked the doors and has announced a delay, due to an animal on the line further on."

Neil was mistaken. Two passengers had watched him get out. They were both regulars and although they had not seen what he had discovered, they knew something was wrong from the shaken appearance of the guard, who they knew quite well as he was often on the same train. The two passengers discussed it.

"What do you think is the matter?"

"From the look on his face, I expect it was a suicide or something like that. I think we should tell him we know something is wrong."

"Yes they might want us to help, or make statement or something. You off to work, Aiden?"

"Yes, Donna, I am. I work at the garage in town just down from the station. I know you go further down the road when we get off the train, but not where to."

"Yes, I work at the ambulance station. I clean there and then go on to the Thistle and Rose as kitchen porter at lunch time."

When they pulled into the Station, they were met by several police officers, who took details of everyone, before they could move onto their respective destinations. Neil was taken into the ticket office where he told the policeman what had happened. His supervisor was there, and Neil was quite proud of the fact he remained calm and coherent in his account. While the policeman was talking to his control room, Neil turned to his supervisor and said, "I knew something bad would happen, I saw the ghost this morning, you know, they call it Suicide Sid, at Skipton. Never seen it before. I even noted it down in the incident log, it's in my pack, here."

Ernie, the supervisor, looked at him with sympathy.

"I saw it once too. Long time ago, mind. When I got home that night, I got a call to say my dad had died of a stroke. I reckons you can stop worrying about your family now, now you knows what it is."

"Thanks, yes, I was worrying a bit, silly really. I never believed it before, like, but I do now. Is John OK? He's only a lad, nice chap, he coped well, but it turned him up."

"One of the ticket staff is making him a brew, I'll get you one, after you have done all the usual breath and urine tests. You knows the score, we has to, to comply with all the rules. We have to be seen to be squeaky clean, you don't mind do you, no objections?"

"Of course not. Pleased to. I suppose this is classed as an incident isn't it? I have nothing to hide, in fact I could do with a leak, can I do it now?"

Neil duly provided the samples and then spoke to the police, and told them what had happened. He and John were accompanied by railway staff to their homes and only when the supervisors were sure they had company, and were all right, did they leave. They were told a CID officer would ring and take detailed statements later.

The first officer at the scene was a shift WPC, from the local police station. Her name was Sandra Lancashire, and she was just out of her two years' probationary service in the police. She had initially called at the college reception, and was met by one of the security officers (who they referred to as college wardens) who accompanied her to the field by the railway line, using the college Land Rover. She knew the warden from the several occasions she had attended the college before for various reasons. She had dealt with a case of damage and another of minor theft, as well as attending in a civilian capacity to watch a couple of rugby games where friends of hers at the college were playing.

As she approached the body she noticed a trail of blood through the grass, and the obvious signs of something or somebody having been dragged through the rough vegetation of the field. Unusually there were no sheep in the field, as it was apparently being used to grow a hay crop. She saw that the body was dead, but still checked. She knew exactly what to do, it was not the first time she had dealt with a sudden death, but never one as serious as this looked to be. She thanked the warden and asked him to return to the college and await her colleagues, and then made sure the scene was not disturbed. As he went back, she called up on her radio, and started an incident log to record everything that happened.

About half an hour later she saw some of her colleagues and the police surgeon approaching from the nearby lane. She meticulously recorded each of them and the time of their arrival. Her sergeant approached her, with the surgeon, who soon pronounced life extinct, signed her sheet, and went back to his car. Her sergeant said, "Are you all right, Sandra? This is a bit grizzly to say the least. Everyone, the whole circus, is on their way. I am afraid you are in for a long day. Do you need owt? No? Well, stay here, keep the log, and let no one near until the Scenes of Crime lads have finished. Do we know who it is?"

"No. I didn't let the warden close enough. I have only confirmed no pulse, and have touched nothing else, but I have been looking. There is a trail of blood there, and tracks, it leads off towards that fence, near that machinery over there, a baler or tractor or something. I have not moved, just looked. Do you think he had an accident and crawled here?"

"Why here, and not back to the college, if he was trying to get help?"

"Maybe he knew the railway phone was here."

"Still seems a bit odd. You are doing a good job, keep it up. The Chief Super from CID is on his way. Have you met him?"

"What Mr Catchpole? Heavens no! I have heard of him, of course, who hasn't? Oh God, I hope I have done it right! I thought it would be the Transport Police. Why him? Now I am scared!"

"Don't worry, you might find him all right. He is a quiet man, very proper. Just don't annoy him. There have been two other suspicious deaths on the railway line recently, and the Transport Police have asked us to deal. One body was on the line about three miles away, and the other just outside town. He is already dealing with those, and they want him to do this one too."

"I thought they were suicides?"

"That is what we were meant to think, but apparently not. Both of them were moved to the line, but were killed elsewhere. Looks like this one was moved too. You will know the Chief Super, tall, red hair, limp. But there is a woman Detective Inspector Allenby works on the squad. I will get you a relief in a bit. Do you need anything? Well done, Sandra, you seem to be on top of things. Anything worrying you? Are you OK on your own here?"

"I am fine, just worried that he will think I am thick or something. I have heard about him."

"You know, you might be pleasantly surprised. We are setting up a small control point in the lane there. I'll get someone to bring you a coffee, white no sugar isn't it?"

Sandra dutifully stayed at her post, logging everything for about two hours. The photographer from Scenes of Crime brought her a coffee and then she saw a tall slim, red-headed man walking towards her from the lane, in a white coverall suit. He was limping slightly. Although she knew who he was she challenged him anyway, just to prove she was conscientious. She timed his arrival on her sheet and in her pocket notebook, and looked up with some trepidation into blue eyes that smiled down at her. He produced his warrant card and said,

"I am Detective Chief Superintendent Saul Catchpole. Who are you?"

"WPC 213 Sandra Lancashire, sir."

"May I see your log please? Thank you. This is excellent, well done. Your skipper says you have observed a blood trail and marks in the grass, please come with me while we check them out."

He turned to another officer and said, "Paul, please take over the log from this officer and stay with the body. I suppose I had better look at it. Yes, not nice. Who was sick? I can smell it from here?"

"Not me, sir, I think it was the guard on the train. No one since I have been here."

As she handed over to Paul and signed the log over, Mr Catchpole looked at the body and carefully glanced all around.

"Right, WPC Lancashire, let's see what we can find, may I call you Sandra?"

"Of course, sir. Why do you need me, I'm just a basic uniform officer, only just out of probation? What can I contribute?"

"So far you have acted with intelligence, diligence and observation. I need your input, unless you would rather not?"

"Please, I would love to be involved if I can, but I am only a shift officer."

"No, officer, you are more than that. You are local, you know a few people here, and the patch. The warden told me."

Sandra looked up into the lined and thin freckled face, and saw the smile again, and his eyes twinkling at her. She saw nothing to be wary of and wondered why he was held in awe by so many officers. He reminded her of a softer, kinder version of her father.

"Now what have you been told that makes you so scared of me, I wonder?"

"Well, nothing, well, not much, anyway, I mean nothing at all, but you are so very senior, and all the CID lads I know talk of you with such respect, like you are a god or something!"

His laugh was real and infectious. As they walked slowly away he chuckled and said, "Let me guess. You have heard I have a temper and can be very tough if I need to be, and I am an old-fashioned bumbling old goat with a sharp tongue and unforgiving disposition. That is about it, isn't it?"

Sandra didn't know quite what to say. She had heard all of that, and more, but thought carefully about her answer.

"I also heard that you nearly died keeping hold of a prisoner once, and that is how you got your limp, and that you hold the Police Bravery Medal for it."

"That may be true, and some of the rest of it, but you, young lady, are very tactful. Do you think this looks like someone crawled or walked in this grass?"

"No, it looks like something or someone has been dragged. Look, there, there is a pen or biro or something, and another item up there, not sure what."

"I agree; you have sharp eyes. Did you look at the injuries on the body?"

"I didn't have much choice, but not closely, no. All I did was make sure he was really dead, I did look but did not touch, except to feel for a pulse. I wouldn't have thought anyone with those massive injuries would have been able to crawl, let alone walk. One of his shoes was missing, I couldn't see it anywhere. If he had crawled, his hands would have been mucky, but they weren't. Bloody, yes, but would grass not have stuck to them?"

"Go on."

He beckoned to some forensic officers to come towards them, and said, "What else did you see?"

"His coat was rucked up. Like he had been dragged along by his feet."

"Well done. What else did you see or hear?"

"How did you know I'd heard anything?"

"You wrote 'funny soft noise' on the log."

"Oh yes, so I did. It was just odd. I put the time too. It was just after I got here, I'd sent the warden back, and I'd looked at the body from where I was stood. I got a funny feeling, thought I was being watched or something. I didn't feel as if I was alone. At first I thought it would be a sheep or animal, then I considered badgers or rabbits or foxes even, but it was like a soft rustling and I distinctly heard a stick crack. It wasn't near, but then I couldn't hear it any more or see anything so I just put it down to being a bit jumpy next to a grizzly corpse, thought it was my imagination. And you will think me nuts but…"

"I doubt it, tell me anyway. I need to know what it is that is worrying you, something is."

"There was a funny smell, very faint, but it was just a whiff. I wish I could explain what it was, but I don't know. It was sort of a very clean smell, and it is not the first time I have smelled it. Not aftershave, well, it might have been, but I think it was something else, I can't explain, not unpleasant certainly. Look, there is something else in the grass, up there in the middle of the tracks."

Saul Catchpole indicated to several officers who were following them, to investigate. Sandra walked slowly beside him, as they approached a gate into a wood, and they were followed by several forensic officers.

"You suggested to Sergeant Cole that the man might have had an accident with this machinery, which if I am not mistaken is a tractor with what I think are baling spikes? "

"Yes it is, and it is covered in blood. That looks like flesh on that spike there."

"I think you are right, but tell me what else do you see?

"There is a frayed rope hanging from the tree above, and there is blood on the wheel of the tractor, but none that I can see on the gate. So the gate must have been opened, while the body was dumped and then dragged through. If he had made his own way the gate would have some blood on it, instead there is a pool. The tractor key is gone, not in the ignition anyway. From what I can see there is no blood in the cab."

"You obviously know more about tractors than I do, should it have a key?"

"Yes, that type does. It is a Zetor, they need one. I was brought up on a farm. My dad had one, but it expired years ago. I used to play on the tractor, as did my brothers. Those spikes, we use them for picking up and transporting the big bales. You know, that rope doesn't make any sense at all, even if it is anything to do with this. Looks rather new. The spikes are not usually so sharp. It takes some force to impale anything except bales. It looks as if he fell on them from some height, but how? If he had then he wouldn't have got himself off, not with the injuries I saw anyway. I'm sorry, sir, I am rambling on, forgive me, ignore me, what do I know?"

"I have no intention of doing anything of the sort. You are thinking on your feet, girl, very well, too. I need to know these things. Do you fancy coming on the squad for a while, to help me with these farming things about which I will admit I know very little?"

"I would love to, sir, but I don't think I will be allowed to. The shift is short enough as it is. I am sure you can find more experienced and more expert officers. I doubt my inspector would let me."

"But you wouldn't mind if he did?"

"She, sir, my inspector is a woman. I'd love to, even if it is just to do the filing and make the tea. I really enjoyed my CID attachment. I was hoping to join CID when I had a bit more service. Now I am just concentrating on getting my promotion exams as soon as I can take them."

Sandra blushed and looked up at him. The Scenes of Crime officers had already arrived and were carefully examining and photographing the scene. Saul Catchpole was watching them with a rather distant look on his face, as if he were thinking of something quite different. He turned and said, "I think your inspector will be delighted to lend you to me. In fact, I know she will. Most officers would have chucked up, or gone green on me by now. Do you have a cast iron stomach?"

"I suppose I have. Dad did quite a lot of butchering on the farm. I got used to blood and guts. Once I knew the man was dead, that was all he was to me, a body. Does that sound callous?"

"Not to me, no. Apart from the warden, do you know anyone at this college?"

"Yes, I do. Several of my brothers' friends are here, and a couple of my neighbours. I even looked at coming here myself but decided farming wasn't really my thing. I am not really a

29

farmer. I can help around a farm of course, but my heart isn't in it. I wanted something different."

"I see. Now Sandra, I would like you to return to Sergeant Cole, go back to your station, have a break, you have certainly earned one, if you are willing, wait for me to get there? I will need you in plain clothes please. What time does your shift finish?"

"Two this afternoon, sir, but I am quite happy to work on."

"Good lass! I'll square it with your inspector and your skipper, don't fret. Not due to go on leave in the near future are you?"

"No, but even if I was I'd cancel it for this opportunity."

"Off you go, and thank you. I'll see you back at the nick."

Chapter Two

Saul quickly organized his team at the college and then drove back to the nearby police station. It was fairly typical of an older station, rather shabby and poorly equipped. He was shown up to the Inspector's office, and sat down at her invitation and she made him a coffee, which he graciously and gratefully accepted. He thanked her and smiled weakly and said, "I am sorry but I need to second WPC Lancashire for a while, I can arrange a replacement for you. She did very well this morning and is an observant young officer. I need her farming knowledge and her quick thinking. Will it make life very awkward for you?"

"Yes, sir, it will. She may be young in service but she is about the best I have. Reliable, thorough, and keen. Of course I want to help, but must you take her? I have three other officers on that shift I would rather lend you."

"Why?"

"They all have more service, but nothing like her work rate. They will also be jealous if she gets it and they don't."

"In other words they are not up to her standard, thanks, but no thanks. I want her because she has ability, and specialist knowledge. You can't palm me off with some lazy or tired officer who thinks longer service entitles them to an easy option, which I can assure you is not what it will be! Nice try!"

"I was afraid of that. Very well, I'll let her go. Now how can I help you?"

"I won't take your office from you, or even use this station, I have asked at the college, they can give me some secure rooms there. I will need some digs locally for at least a few days until things have calmed down. Any suggestions? Celia Allenby will be liaising with the welfare matters and all that, do you know her?"

"Yes, I do, we have been on a couple of courses together, I suggest you book into the Lucky Horse Shoe B&B just down the road from the college. It is clean, and the food is a bit basic, but home cooked and very good. Several of my relatives have stayed there in the past. I knew this would happen, you always second someone from the local station, why?"

"Yes, I usually do. I find it helpful. Not only do they have local knowledge, but I find it tends to oil the wheels between the local station and my team. Of course there can be friction, when we come in and take over. It is Lorraine, isn't it? You were a skipper at Skipton for a while?"

"Yes I am surprised you remember me. That was a few years ago."

"I seldom forget a pretty woman, or a good officer."

Lorraine Bradley laughed.

"I remember you! Flattery will get you nowhere. You worked on that nasty case when that child was killed, young Mohammed Aziz. You managed to get the whole Asian community working with you. I often wondered how."

"Yes, I remember. I will tell you how, but not now. Hopefully I can chew the fat with you later, I must get things going on this case. Any time now, I expect the British Transport Police will arrive and I can liaise with them, they have already requested we take this case on."

"Is it connected with the other two deaths?"

"I suspect so, both were made to look like suicide, and both have a connection with farming, and they ended up on the line as well. I would like any thoughts you may have on that, or your officers may have. Neither of them were on your patch."

"No, that's true, one was just over the boundary in the next division, the other miles away, but I believe their relatives live on my patch. Let me know what else you require. We are only a small station, but if we can help, we will."

*

Saul drove back to the college with Sandra and two other members of his team. He was met by his deputy, Celia Allenby. As they all walked into the college reception, he said,

"Celia, this is WPC Sandra Lancashire. I've seconded her. How far have you got?"

"We have been given a wing of the college that is unused, to ourselves, sir. We think we know who the man is, he answers the description of the Sheep Tutor here, a Michael Grady. He has been missing since early last night. His car is in the car park here and his wife rang a short while ago to see if he had stayed over here last night, after some sort of tutorial. He does sometimes. Actually there was no tutorial, but she obviously thought there was."

"Why do we think it is him, we will need more than that."

"I know. He had some ID in his pockets and he is the only man of that description here at college."

"What has the wife been told?"

"Nothing yet. Shall I go and see her?"

"Not yet, let's not pre-empt things."

Saul went into an office and quickly read through the logs and some documentation that had already been obtained. Most of his team were out taking statements from potential witnesses. He called Sandra into the office.

"Have you made your statement yet?"

"Yes, sir, I have just finished it. Here it is. I produced the log as an exhibit, as DI Allenby told me, and put in everything I could. Now what do you want me to do?"

"I would like you to start by talking to the canteen staff here. I have discovered that good folk such as them usually know everything that goes on about everybody in such an establishment, as do the cleaners. I need you to listen, chat and be friendly. Start by handing over this cash and getting us a tab for teas and meals, and please get a receipt. Can you do that, without telling them any details?"

"Sure I can, do you want anything now, a bacon butty or something? I will get a receipt for everything."

"I would love a coffee, white no sugar, but I don't eat pork or bacon, anything else will be fine. Come to think of it I am hungry, are you not?"

"Yes, sir, I am, ravenous, I am afraid. I was so busy and then so excited I forgot about eating. Is a cheese sandwich all right?"

"Yes, fine, I have arranged that we will be billed for all the meals but use that cash to start it off. Incidentally, use it to get yourself something now, on me, you have been a great help to me already. It is the least I can do. A proper meal that is. If you hear anything about the Sheep Tutor, Mike Grady or connected in any way to him, tune in and listen please. Find out all the gossip that must be rife in a place like this."

"Sure, but I already know about him, never met him mind, but I have heard he is a sexist and rather unpleasant chap. A friend of mine was here last year and she loathed him, said he deliberately marked her down all the time. Only hearsay of course. He is a womanizer too, according to what I've been told. Is that who our corpse is? From what I've heard I wouldn't be surprised. When I can tell my friend I think she will be delighted."

"Well, you can't tell her yet. We don't know it's him, yet."

"It's all right, I won't say anything until you say I can. Right one mega cheese sandwich and a fish and chips with mushy peas coming up."

"Actually, can you make that two fish and chips and mushy peas and forget the cheese sandwich?"

"I'll bring it back to you so you can eat it here, sir."

Saul watched her as she walked purposefully out of the door and wondered how many years it would be before she had his job. He was very impressed with her and vowed to get her on his team for as long as he could and as soon as he could. He walked into the staff room next door and was met by the College principal. Together they went to Grady's office and looked round. The principal sank onto the chair behind the desk, put his head in his hands and almost sobbed.

"This is a nightmare. Thankfully, just at the moment the Sheep course are on leave, having just completed their second spell of lambing attachments on various farms in the area. All bar a couple, that is. We have several foreign students here on courses, the Sheep Course included, who have nowhere else to go. They have no duties as such until next week, when the whole course should be back. Two students, I know, have remained on the farms having either been asked or offered to stop on for their break, to help out there. The two best ones actually, our two most mature students."

"So, who is here at the moment?"

"There are two Irish lads on the course. One of them is here or should be, and a Canadian girl. One lass is living about ten miles away, she isn't resident. Two on the course are local, so I presume at home. The lad from the Cotswolds may have gone home or might be staying with our local lad, they are good friends. Another chap is at home in Scotland with his family. That is just Mike's main course. The other courses he teaches are mostly in residence. Several from one of the junior courses are covering for the sheep course, helping our shepherd, Nick Greenwood. I know Mike wasn't exactly popular but I cannot imagine anyone wanting to kill him!"

"Why not popular?"

"We have had a lot of complaints about him, both direct and indirect. Some of them about him in particular, and some general. I only took over here a couple of months ago, because the last principal left, in a hurry. I have been trying to put things right. There were several substantive complaints from the female students about blatant sexism and bullying by Mike and the college in general. There were and are allegations that

Mike has doctored the marks of the female students to mark them down, and strangely enough marked up one male student in particular. I think he didn't like female students, or those he didn't consider to be from farming backgrounds. He denies it, of course but something is sadly wrong. I haven't got to the bottom of it yet."

"Go on."

"All the tutors teach almost every student for something. When you have glowing reports from all but one of them about a student, except from Mike, who just gives them a poor pass in all his subjects when they get distinction in everything else, it doesn't add up. Then the opposite, one of the male sheep students has consistently had shocking marks, combined with intermittent attendance at lectures, I wondered why Mike gave him a credit. I asked Mike two weeks ago for all their written work so I could assess it myself, but he has not yet given it to me. One of the Irish lads has been a problem since he arrived. He is disqualified from driving, which we only recently found out, and he has been in trouble for dealing drugs at least twice, and I have been told, but have no proof, that he deals them here in the college. I was intending to get to the bottom of it next week when he is back, with a view to chucking him out. Then I discovered Mike knew about it and had been trying to cover for him. He knew he was disqualified certainly, and let him keep his car here, and take it out. Mike and I had a blazing row about it only two days ago. I suppose that makes me a suspect? It is Mike you have found isn't it?"

"We are not sure. We need to get the body identified, but it looks like it. Exactly what was said between you?"

"Basically Mike said he didn't believe it of Eddie, and thought the report was malicious. One of the other students, one of the mature ones who is still away, hates this lad, I think with good reason. Mike said the woman was trying to cause trouble for Eddie. Mike chose to look at it this way, but I have discovered she is quite right. I have enough evidence to prove it now. I said if I could find out in only a matter of a couple of weeks then he should have been aware of it. Then there is the little matter of the lad's ex-girlfriend, who he had been knocking about when she tried to leave him. I think that basic justice was done over that, the girl, Zoe, she had a lot of friends. Why Eddie was covered in bruises a few days after they split up I don't know. I will tell you I heard that Eddie and Mike had a big falling-out last week, I heard them shouting at each other in an office just down the corridor. It is usually unoccupied and no one ever goes there. I know that Nick our shepherd and Mike had a row too. That was heard by almost everyone down in the sheep sheds. Before I could stop it Mike had stormed off up to the main block. After months of lambing, tempers do get frayed, and a lot of things are said, not always meant, but this was a bit over the top. Do you want me to identify the body, I will, if only to save Mike's wife distress?"

"How kind: I am sure she will be very upset. Yes, please. I warn you, it isn't pretty."

"Oh, I doubt it. All has not been well on that count for some time either. Rumour, and that is all that it is, has it that he had a lady friend here on the staff, a mistress and his wife also had a lover. He did seem to stay over here a lot."

"Who has access to the tractors and farm machinery?"

"The staff of course and the maintenance students, and for most of the vehicles some of the students. Oh yes, one student has authority to drive everything on the campus, which is more than I do. She has a lot of driving experience in her previous profession. She has actually been very useful, we employ her as a driver quite often, as well as in the bar and sometimes she helps the wardens out!"

"Why?"

"She is an ex-police officer, reliable and rather straight-laced. I expect that is why she disliked Eddie so much. She can be very direct at times."

"Who is this ex-officer?"

"Diana Green. Not the easiest of women, she calls a spade a spade, but on everything I have investigated so far, I have found her to be accurate if rather prickly about it. She told me straight that if I didn't sort things out, stop the bullying and the corruption and sexism, then not only would she leave and demand her tuition fees back, she would raise hell with OFSTED about the place. I believe her! She can be quite charming, very reasoned, and quite terrifying on occasion."

"Is she one of those whose marks have been doctored by Grady?"

"Yes. She has at least credits or distinctions in everything else but he has just given her poor passes in all his subjects. One of her assignments was selected to represent the college in a national competition. The independent assessor picked it and re-graded it from Mike's mark of fifty-four percent, to a much more accurate one of ninety-eight percent. The assessor is re-marking all the assignments that Mike was responsible for marking."

"It sounds as if she hates Grady."

"She says not, that she despises him, and actually feels sorry for him. She agrees she has the right to feel aggrieved as do many others, but she said if I dealt with it, she will stay the course, and get the marks she deserves in spite of him. Others hate him more you know, with good reason. I served him a written warning yesterday, and as it isn't here I presume he read it."

"If he was killed, who would you suspect first?"

"The sheep course, en-mass, the shepherd, the husband of whoever he is seeing, his wife, a fair few staff he has upset, other students, the cowman, general farm hands, and even some from the Equine and Arboriculture and Horticulture departments. Our Farm secretary doesn't like him at all, I am not sure why. I haven't been here long enough to find out everything. The last principal and he were great pals, and when your lot arrested my predecessor for fraud, I got the impression that Grady was suspected too. The college governors are in despair. They think the place will have to close if we don't get it sorted out. You do know what is due to happen here next month? The new Equestrian unit is being opened, and the new dairy unit. We are expecting thousands. The EU has funded the whole thing, it is to be a show piece, and some very important national figures and heads of state are going to officiate at the opening, even royalty, ours, of course. Now this, this might be the straw that breaks the camel's back!"

"I had heard. Yes, I do know it has been planned for a long time. Who have you been liaising with over security?"

"Your Assistant Chief Constable 'Operations' Gaskell, nice chap!"

"Don't despair yet, I will happily talk to your governors. Tell me, do you know or have you heard of either Dominic McGill or William Birtwhistle?"

"'Yes, I have, they are both from farming families that take our students for various attachments. Why?"

"Because both have been killed in the last two months, we believe murdered."

"I had heard one had died. Are you saying this is connected with them?"

"Probably, it is the first time I have had a link between them. Neither really knew each other."

"If we have a serial killer here, should I close the college?"

"No not yet. I will work with you on this, Professor Hardaker, if you will help me."

"I need all the help I can get. How did you know I was a professor, that is not known here?"

"I am a detective it is my job to find out things, I looked you up before I came out here. Who can tell me where I can find all these students, as a starter?"

"Rachel, our secretary, I have told her to help you in any way. She has probably already typed it up for you. She is very efficient. Shall I go and identify Mike, and then I will go and talk to Susan his wife. If you want?"

"Thank you, yes, will you go with DI Allenby now?"

Saul had a very busy day, and it was late in the afternoon when he called in at his B&B.

He was greeted by a middle-aged lady smelling faintly of lavender and baking. He smiled and said, "Good evening, I am Saul Catchpole and I believe my Police Headquarters booked me in here for a few nights."

"Indeed they did, Mr Catchpole. Your room is ready. I'm Eileen Roberts and my husband is called Tom. I hopes you don't mind the dog around. Your people said they didn't think you would. It don't go into the dining room, and there is your own sitting room if you wants to use it, but you are more than welcome to sit in our lounge. The dog is allowed in there with us. I am afraid we don't do no fancy food like those posh hotels, and your office says you can't eat pork, is there anything else you don't like? I went and got some vegetarian sausages for your breakfast."

"How kind of you, and I much prefer good home-cooked food. You come highly recommended you know."

"Well, I never! I didn't know we was known by the coppers. What a compliment. Here is your room. It is en suite. Is you really an important detective?"

"Detective yes, not that important, I am, after all, just a copper. This is a lovely house. How tastefully you have decorated it. Can I leave my bag here? I will be out most of the time. I will have to lock a lot of paperwork away, will it be safe in this room?"

"Quite safe, both the chest of drawers and wardrobe have keys and no one will come in. I will be here most of the time. Have you time for a meal now?"

"I am afraid not. These are my keys? Is one for the front door in case I have to go out suddenly?"

"Yes, dearie, that one"

Saul made an instant hit when he made firm friends with the small poodle and said how handsome it was. Eileen smiled at him.

"His name is Roy. You like dogs?"

"Yes I do, I have two Labradors at home. I like cats too. Do you have any?"

"Yes two, one big marmalade, and one tabby. Is something going on at the college?"

"Yes, I am afraid so."

"I used to work in the kitchens there. So did Tom, in maintenance. If you want to know anything about the place, we might be able to help you. We both retired a couple of years ago. I get to hear a lot of the gossip still. I can tell you lots about the last principal and the goings-on there. One of the staff on the agricultural lot, he books in here sometimes, but it ain't his wife, that I do know. It ain't our business, he always pays but I don't like the man at all. I know who the woman is married to and it isn't him, but we is in business after all so we takes his money."

"Do you know the man's name?"

"He calls himself Murphy, but I know he is Grady, something to do with the sheep I think. He came to the college just after we retired. You off out again? Let yourself in if we is in bed. I'll not wait up for you. Your people said you might be out a lot."

Saul spent the evening reading statements, and documentation. He had spoken to the pathologist and knew he was dealing with another murder. All his team worked late into the evening with him and he made it back to his lodgings just before midnight. Eileen had left a chicken salad out for him which he ate and what he could not manage, the dog and two cats happily assisted him with, assuring him they loved chicken too. His room was warm and the bed spotless and very comfy. He was asleep in minutes.

Chapter Three

Although Saul was up early, Eileen was before him and had cooked him a huge breakfast which she insisted he needed, and once he had eaten it, she handed him a thermos and a packed lunch. He realized he had been adopted by her when he saw she had included a couple of carefully wrapped sweets and some chocolate biscuits. She asked if his room was comfortable and he assured her it was and said, "I will be out most of the day, but I do need to talk to you and Tom about what you know at the college."

She said, "You'll fade away if you don't eat regular. I heard what happened, and I knows you'll be busy. I'm out shopping today, do you want me to get you owt? Me and Tom will be in this evening. Talk to us then, and I knows we don't have a licence but share a glass of wine or a beer with us then, you will be most welcome."

"I will. The room is so comfy, I can even do my paperwork in there. Thank you."

As he drove the short distance to the agricultural college he felt most refreshed and appreciated the joys of an excellent shower in his bathroom, and the benefits of a good breakfast. Having stopped off at the offices at the college he went on and attended the post-mortem of Grady, who had been identified the previous evening by Professor Hardaker. The pathologist was, as usual, very cautious about anything not glaringly obvious, but was as helpful as she could be. Saul had an excellent relationship with her because he never pressed her to say anything she couldn't prove and knew if he waited she would be meticulous in any investigation. On this occasion he left armed with a great deal of information and then returned, calling all of his team back to the office for a briefing. While he waited for them to arrive he read through all the new paperwork. They soon assembled and he shut the door of the room and said, "This is what we know so far. The deceased was Michael John Grady, originally O'Grady, born in Newcastle West, Eire. He came with his family to England when he was three, but returned in his late teens and early twenties to Dublin and County Wexford. An intelligent man, he had a degree in Animal Nutrition, obtained at a college in Ireland. He worked his way through various college posts until he was appointed head lecturer and Sheep Tutor here two and a half years ago. He has a wife and one step daughter, who is in her teens. He was killed between midnight and two in the morning he was found. He did not die where his body was found; he actually died on the baler spikes of the tractor at the edge of the wood. His body was removed and dragged to the edge of the railway embankment. As far as we can make out he fell from the tree above onto the spikes and there were marks on the body indicating he had been tied and gagged. Who found the other bit of the rope in the woods? Thank you, Julie, well done. Here is the strange bit. The rope was eaten through with acid, probably battery acid, we have yet to get the lab results. It looks like he was tied, gagged and suspended above the baler and then acid was applied to the rope, causing it to break when he would have fallen onto the spikes, and been impaled. His death was not instantaneous either. Then, after a while, quite a while actually, someone unknown removed him and dragged him across the field and put him over the fence into the ditch."

Saul paused while the team took in the horrific implications of what he had said. Someone mentioned, "That's barbaric, it must have been someone who hated him very much, very personal."

"Yes I agree, the thing we know about this killer, at the moment is this, he or she, or even they, are cruel, evil and very strong and they are connected with here or with Grady himself. The last sighting of the tractor was about nine the night before, and the extra couple of miles since the last log book entry have not been signed for. The shepherd and one student from the basic farm course moved a couple of dead sheep to the pit in the tractor box and put the tractor in the barn by nine. The baler spikes were on the tractor then, in fact the shepherd used them to fetch a bale of straw on his way back to the barn from the pit. You have all been wonderful getting as much information as you have. Sandra, you made quite a hit with the kitchen staff, and got a lot of information. I am impressed! Our next job is to talk to the students, especially the ones on the Sheep course who had most to do with Grady. Celia, you and I will go and visit this Diana Green, it is a fair drive. I want the rest of you to pair up and take the other students in turn. Geoff, can you organize that? Did we locate this Eddie?"

"No, not yet. Although he is supposed to be here on campus, he told someone he was heading down to London for a few days. My informants tell me that means he has gone to get a new supply of drugs, something he does quite often. The Canadian girl is here though, she is helping the shepherd down in the sheep unit."

"Thanks, Tarik, you and Sandra talk to her. If anyone won't cooperate, nick them, but I doubt that will be necessary. Oh, and I want DNA samples from everyone."

"Sir, surely we are looking for a man for this? I doubt any woman would have been strong enough?"

A snort of laughter came from Sandra.

"Julie, I am reliably informed that any shepherd has to be strong, and all of the students on this course are so, and very fit. They can turn over, control and treat these massive sheep they have here. What kind of sheep are they here, Sandra?"

"Suffolks, Mules, mainly, with a few Texels, and a dozen or so Blue Faced Leicesters, and a couple of Wensleydales, and I am told a Leicester Longwool or so. They can weigh up to one hundred and twenty kilograms."

"You see everyone, we mustn't prejudge. And we are looking at every and anyone. Or even several!"

David, one of the Detective Constables, turned to Geoff, his sergeant, and said, "If the girls here can do that, yes I see. Quite frightening, when you think of it."

Sandra, who was sitting next to them muttered, "It is not for nothing that the first shepherd was called Abel."

David said, "I don't understand."

Geoff said, "It is in the Bible, Adam, the first man, had three sons, the first was Cain, a tiller of the soil. The second was Abel who was a shepherd. Cain killed Abel, and the third was much younger and was called Seth."

David paused, and then said, "Oh, I see. So we are looking for a man called Cain?"

Everyone laughed and Saul said, "Yes in a way I suppose we are. There for I am proposing that we call this operation, Operation Cain, everyone agree?"

The meeting broke up and all went off to their allotted tasks, and Saul and Celia set off for the drive up to the hills.

*

In a remote dale, high up. Diana was working with her dog in one of the lambing fields, which was either side of the road leading to the farm. The farmer, Jim, was working back in the farmyard by the buildings. Diana was checking all the twins born that day and had just put several ewes and lambs into holding pens when she noticed a car drive down the road towards the farm buildings. Assuming it was a visitor for Jim she carried on with her work. She called her dog, a very large white-faced border collie called Drift, to her, and wondered as strangers seldom visited and very few came in any vehicle other than a four-wheel drive. She moved on and gathered another group of ewes and moved them up the hill. It took concentration for both her and the dog and she finally headed them into the next pasture with their lambs and paused to catch her breath. Drift waited expectantly for the next command.

"Lie down, steady, steady, good dog. Right, hold them, lay down."

She closed the gate to the paddock and patted the dog in appreciation of a task well performed. Drift gave a low and soft growl and Diana turned and saw the same car that had passed earlier parked on the road and a tall slim man and a woman, walking up the slope towards her. They were not dressed for country pursuits and then she noticed Jim coming up the hill on his quad behind them.

She secured the pen and walked to meet them.

"Hello, who are you? You do know this is not a right of way? Why are you here? You are not exactly dressed for country walking."

"Diana Green? I am a police officer. Detective Chief Superintendent Saul Catchpole. This is DI Allenby. We need to talk to you."

"Do you? What is this about? You would hardly trail out here unless it was important. How can I help you?"

"Would you mind coming down to the police station so we can talk there?"

"Yes, I would, very much, but I can see that you need to talk to me about something. All right, but I will have to ask Jim, and I am needed here. He will have to take my dog back with him. Do you suspect me of something? I have nothing to hide and have done nothing wrong. What is this about?"

Jim, who had pulled up by them on his quad, said, "Are you all right, Di?"

"I suppose so, but they want to take me down the nick. I think they suspect me of something. I'll have to go with them. Could you look after Drift? I'll be back as soon as I can. There is a ewe up by the standing stone that is due to lamb any minute now, and one that just has, over there by the scree slope under the long wall. Look, I have no money on me, can I go up to the farm and get changed and get my things?"

"I'd rather you came now, don't worry we will bring you back, I wouldn't ask if it was not important and rather urgent."

"And if I don't agree to come I think you will arrest me anyway?"

"Probably."

"Why?"

"I am investigating the murder of a Michael Grady. I think you may be able to assist me."

"Tigger? He's dead? Yes, I see why you might want to talk to me. OK. I'll come, if that's all right with you, Jim? I don't smell too good, and would prefer to have a shower first but if it is that urgent you will have to put up with the smell."

"I'd rather do it now."

"Very well, Jim, could you take Drift for me? If I am not back in a couple of hours ring the police station. Where are you taking me?"

"Skipton."

"Make that four hours, Jim."

"Do you want me to come too, Di, I don't want anyone to take advantage."

"I might want you to, but they don't, I can tell. Don't worry, I think I'll be all right. I've done nothing wrong, so hopefully I have nothing to fear. Look, there is a weak lamb, one of twins in the pen there. The other is enormous I was going to lift it later if it was in trouble. I have marked it, green dot on the back of the neck."

"Di, who shall I tell about this?"

"I think these two would rather you didn't make a fuss, but if you haven't heard by supper time, tell the farm manager Donald."

As they walked down the hill, Diana smiled gently to herself when Celia Allenby stepped in some sheep droppings and then into a large and muddy puddle. She was wearing some rather fashionable heeled patent black leather shoes. Saul, Diana noticed, was wearing wellington boots but was otherwise dressed in a very beautifully tailored suit. Diana walked over to a large rock by the road and picked up a small rucksack from on top of it and said, "Do you want to search me first?"

Saul looked down at her and smiled slightly. "Could you put the bag and the contents of your pockets and your coat in this bag please, we will lock it in the boot for the journey. I think you know the score."

Diana nodded and took off her jacket, rolled it in a ball and placed it in the large plastic bag that Celia had produced from the boot, and then Diana emptied her numerous trouser pockets. Saul looked in amazement at the contents of the pockets and caught a mischievous grin from Diana.

"Shepherds have a lot of pockets, usually full of all sorts of things, knives, syringes, spray cans, twine, and some quite disgusting things get in there too. Oh, here, ma'am, a couple of tissues to wipe your townie shoes. Some of these things can be rather dangerous in the wrong hands. My phone is in the rucksack but it is turned off. There, I think that's it, no, I was wrong, there are some castrating rings here and the applicator, I'd forgotten them, I expect you would like to search me."

Celia patted Diana down and said, "Thanks for that. We just need to check you have no weapons on you."

"Yes I understand that. I assure you I have nothing like that."

Diana got into the back seat of the car and the journey took some time. The only time Diana said anything was to direct them at a junction, when Celia was not sure which turning to take. At the station she was taken to an interview room and invited to sit down. Saul looked down at Diana and said,

"What time did you start this morning?"

"About half four."

"Do you want a cup of tea?"

"Yes, please, I'm parched, I was just going in for a bite and a drink when you arrived. You suspect me of murder don't you?"

"What makes you think that?"

"Well, your rank for one thing. Anyone of your high rank doesn't deal with petty things. You have told me Tigger was killed. The urgency with which you need to deal with this. If I were just a witness, however important, you would have interviewed me at the small police station a few miles from the farm or even at the farm house. Therefore, you suspect me. I expect just at the moment the lady officer with you is either cleaning off her shoes or searching through my belongings before bringing them in here. She should be careful, one of the syringes has pus in it I took from an abscess earlier today. I was going to chuck it. I think you should warn her that she should have nothing to do with sheep if she is pregnant, they can carry spontaneous abortion."

"You are being very calm about this, and remarkably lacking in curiosity."

"You wouldn't tell me anything you didn't want me to know, even if I did press you for it. If Grady was killed, I know just why I would be a suspect, as I have as much motive for wanting him out of my hair as most people who know him, but I can assure you it wasn't me. I will help you as much as I can."

"Will you? I think you might help us as much as you want to, and no more."

"True. Are you going to caution me?"

"In due course. I would like to tape any interview we have with you."

"Am I under arrest?"

"No, you are free to go if you insist."

"No, I'm not. As long as I cooperate we will pretend I am here of my own volition. If I stop helping you, then things will change. Actually, I don't mind helping you and the sooner the better. I'll even give you permission to search my things, although I think that is a bit late now, if you need to. I have nothing to hide from you. I happen to be innocent but it looks like I might have to prove it."

The civil but thinly disguised hostility between them alerted Saul to the fact that she was a very clever woman and that it was not going to be an easy task to discover exactly what she knew. She sat patiently in the interview room sipping the tea she had been brought and then he went and found Celia. The camera from the interview room showed that Diana seemed to be totally at ease and utterly unconcerned. Any attempt to intimidate or frighten her were not going to work.

He wondered why. He found Celia frantically cleaning off her shoes and he smiled wryly to himself that Diana could read his colleague so easily. He said, "Have you searched through her things yet?"

"Well, yes, I did have a quick look. I know, we are supposed to get her permission, but there might be dangerous things in there like she said. There was a syringe with some yellow drug in it. Shall I seize it and send it for analysis?"

"She knew you would do this and has given me retrospective permission. I think you might find the contents of that syringe is pus and it would be better disposed of, she has also said to do that with it. This is a very clever woman, Celia, and we must be very careful; to say she is beginning to annoy me is an understatement. I am missing something, important, and I don't know what. Have you done a check on her?"

"Yes, it is rather odd. No trace at all. Nothing, like the woman doesn't actually exist. Yes, her driving licence, with an address in Somerset is genuine, and totally clean, and covers her for HGVs, PCVs and bikes as well as various quite unusual things, but there is nothing else. Her National Insurance number comes back in her name but I happen to know it is a fairly recently issued one, like she had been out of the country or something, there is no passport in her things. Her phone won't turn on without a password. It is a very heavy phone. Got a very big battery."

Saul realized this was going to be more challenging. Diana Green was calm and unafraid. She knew too much about the system to be intimidated, or frightened, and he needed to be very clever. He went with Celia into the interview room, and asked, "Do you need to use the cloakroom before we start?"

"How kind of you, yes, I do. I expect this lady would like to accompany me?"

Diana stood up and the two women left the room to go down the corridor to the toilets. Saul sat thinking how to approach the matter and gave a cursory glance around the room to see if anything had been dropped. The only strange thing was a single piece of plain paper that had been neatly torn into strips and when he looked at how they had been placed he thought they were laid on the table as if to spell 00. The two women returned and he noticed that Celia had obviously taken the opportunity to wash her hands, as they were still damp.

The interview began and Celia started the tape machine. Saul cautioned Diana, and asked her full name.

"Diana Green, born 12.11.56 in London."

"Have you ever had any other name?"

"No."

"What is your occupation?"

"Student shepherd."

"Are you an ex-police officer?"

"Yes."

"What force?"

"Wiltshire."

"Where were you for the last seventy-two hours?"

"At Moorside Farm where you found me. I've been there for three weeks, more, four actually. In the last three days I left the farm once, the day before yesterday. I went to the village, Hebden, and purchased some smokes from the post office and general store there, for me and Jim. The receipt is still in my purse. I took my car. I was gone a couple of hours. I left about four in the afternoon and got back just before six. When I got back, Jim had gone out, over to friends at Leyburn I think, to see his brother who has been poorly. He got back late, about three a.m. I think. I had to be up about half four, so he had a lay in, so I didn't see him till a lot later, about nine a.m. I know this means I don't have an alibi for all the time, but then I didn't know I would need one. The rest of the time, Jim, or Donald can vouch for me."

"How did you know I was interested in that time?"

"I didn't. That is the only time I have left the farm in five days."

"Why didn't you like Mike Grady?"

"He was a sexist arrogant bigot, and I suspect corrupt. He was unfair, and although a good teacher I think he was a woman-hater, but also a womanizer. I happen to know he was having an affair with a woman at college. That is not any of my business but I've met his wife and rather like her. He was doctoring all the marks of at least the female students on the course and I think one of the male ones, who he has consistently marked up, so he could keep him on the course, for some reason. If he hadn't, the chap would have been chucked out ages ago. Grady didn't like it because I challenged him about it, and stood up to him. I'm paying quite a bit to be on this course and I'll be damned if an arsehole like that is going to rob me of fair marks, and a qualification I deserve. I don't want any favours, just recognition of what I have achieved. Naturally he resented it, and has made life very difficult for me. When I refused to do all the filthy jobs all the time, and extra farm duties that it was not my turn to do, I told him to stop trying to force me off the course, and it wasn't going to work. I told him I wasn't afraid of him and I had my own methods of defence."

"Tell me, are you afraid of anything or anybody? When did you last see him?"

"To the first question, I don't know, to the second, two weeks ago, when he came to visit me on the farm and three weeks before that when he visited me at my last placement, over on the lowland farm. He asked me then if I would withdraw my complaint against him. I refused."

"What was his reaction?"

"He said I would regret it, and I would fail anyway, as I had dreadful marks. He came a bit unstuck, because the farmer there, who happens to be a very prominent man in farming, both locally and nationally, said he didn't agree, and he intended to give me an excellent assessment for the work I had done. I have a copy of it, which the farmer gave me. I know Mike doctored it but he didn't know I had one. When I saw Mike a fortnight ago, I warned him to stop trying to harass me, and he had underestimated my resolve and intelligence. I suggested he back off and concentrate on getting himself out of the pooh he was already in. We had a bit of a row, and he left. Jim heard it all, he was in the next room. Donald was there too."

"What pooh? Was it more than he was doing to you?"

"Yes. Much more. I'm not a fool. I can see what is going on around me. I know he was being investigated for something to do with the last principal of the college, some sort of fraud. I listen to talk around me, especially while working in the

58

college bar. Mike Grady thought he was invincible, that no one had the knowledge or guts to challenge him. He was wrong. Quite a few hate his guts. At the last farm, one of the shepherds there was on the same course last year, and hated his guts every bit as much as I did. Grady did not expect opposition from a woman. Most of the students are young and easily intimidated. I'm not."

Celia asked, "Did you just have blood on your hands?"

"Yes. Quite a lot of it, fresh this morning. I washed most of it off just now. You will find a lot on my coat as well. I skinned a lamb this morning, it can be a bloody business. You will also find my blood, and some of Jim's on my coat. He cut himself the day before yesterday, and I did a couple of days before, and I got kicked in the mouth by a ewe yesterday. I washed the coat about ten days ago, when we had that fine spell. It is sadly in need of another wash."

"Where is your home?"

"I don't have one, at the moment. I do own a farm here in the Dales, which I rent out. When I have finished this course I shall settle down there, but until then, I'm sort of in limbo. I do have some things in store with a friend down in the Brecon Beacons, and you have my permission to search anything of mine. In Wales, my friend is storing a whole case of documentary evidence about the college and will not release it unless I ask him to. I will ring him and explain if you want me to. Incidentally, on my other jacket, back at college in my room you will find some of Mike's blood. He caught his hand in a gate, on a practical, just before I came away, and I patched him up and took him to hospital. He bled all over me. It is the red canvas jacket. He bled over Nick the shepherd too."

"Why did you take him to the hospital if you dislike him so much?"

"Because I am one of the few who can drive the college car. I may not like the man, but I wouldn't see him suffer, physically that is. It was either me or the shepherd and he was needed to supervise the other students putting the sheep through the footbath. It needs someone in authority, because of the chemicals involved. Mike could be quite pleasant if he wanted to be. He actually thanked me. I've been a first-aider for many years."

"Why did you refer to him as Tigger?"

"He bounced a lot. Full of energy and pomposity. We nicknamed him that when we first arrived."

"Tell me about the other students on your course."

"All right. Alison is Canadian. She liked Mike about as much as I did. He was doctoring her marks too. She is highly intelligent and very strong-willed. Janet, she is the best student in the college. She is shy and rather easily cowed, but she is damn good working with sheep. She puts in loads of extra hours and works very hard. Amy is young, a farmer's daughter. Very strong physically but utterly motivated by her religion, she is naive and a bit obstinate. She is the baby on the course but there is no harm in her. Ruth I hardly know. I don't understand her at all, also very clever, but I'm not sure what she wants with the course, or even what she is doing on it. Very insular. Steve, one of the Irish lads, he goes walkabout, mentally and physically sometimes, and can be a bit odd, but nice enough. Not over bright I don't think, and does not like Amy, because she tries to preach religion to him. Alex is sound as a pound, local farmer quite bright, very mature, good sportsman. Strong as an ox. He lets everything slide past him. As does David, also strong, who is very bright, and pleasant and kind and quiet. Then there is Peter the Scot. We call him Haggis. Not the most literate of lads but willing. Totally motivated by what is between his legs, impulsive and the world's worst driver!"

"You have left out Eddie."

"Yes I know. I'm not quite sure what to say about him. I can't stand the man. I have my reasons. He is utterly evil, I think. He can charm if he wants to, but he is a crook. He also deals drugs, has a violent and mean personality, and he schemes. He seems to have a lot of money periodically. Mainly spent in the bar. He drinks Southern Comfort. He plans nasty little tricks and enjoys hurting things. The sheep, anything that upsets him. I refused, some time ago, to be alone with him, and told Mike I wouldn't work with him. Eddie has tried to set me up several times with 'accidents'. He hates me more than I hate him. He isn't thick, quite the reverse. I couldn't prove it, but he tried to run me over with the tractor not once but twice. We all carry knives, it's part of the job, but he has one concealed in his boot, a huge one. He drew it on me one evening down in the sheep shed, when I told him to stop kicking an ewe that had upset him. Why he is still on the course I don't know. I think he has some sort of hold over Mike. He got pulled over in his car not long ago, and done for no documents. He was convinced I grassed him up. I hadn't but he vowed he would get me for it. I explained, in front of several others, that I had no need to, it was inevitable he would get caught sooner or later. He beat his girlfriend, Zoe, up when she woke up to what an utter shit he was. I think Alex might have sorted him out over that. I like Zoe. I do know that the next day Alex had an accident in the tractor, the brakes had been disconnected. Fortunately, Alex wasn't hurt. No one could prove anything. If anyone is capable of murder, he is. Have you spoken to him?"

"Not yet, he took off to London yesterday. I understand he goes there a lot."

"Yes he does, down to Tilbury, I believe, but not this time. I happen to know where he is at the moment, approximately."

"How?"

"I spoke to someone who knows him, this morning on the phone. They wanted to warn me he was nearby. He did a lambing attachment three valleys over and the farm up the road here is the hill farm for that place. I am friendly with the shepherd's wife up the road, and her cousin is the farmer's wife. He topped himself recently, I tried to do what I could to help her when she stayed for a few days. She disliked Eddie, and knew I did, she thought he was out to cause me trouble. She rang me this morning to tell me he is around the village. I doubt he will come up to our farm but fore warned is fore armed."

"Are you talking about Mr Mc Gill?"

"Yes, such a nice man. I was really upset when I heard about him. He left two lovely kids as well as his wife Gillian. I met him a couple of times, we did some practicals there earlier this year, you know, foot trimming, dagging. He seemed a kind man, very straight."

"Excuse my ignorance, what is dagging?"

"Trimming round sheep's dirty bums. I do know that he sent Eddie home after a couple of weeks, don't know why, they had some sort of falling out. Gillian can tell you. When Mike came to see me two weeks ago he had just been there, to talk to Gillian. He actually asked me what I knew about the affair but I didn't tell him anything because all I knew was hearsay."

"I can tell you, Mr Mc Gill's death was not suicide. We have recently discovered it was murder."

Diana looked at Saul and then thought for a while. She went rather pale and then said, "I see. Yes, I know the family, not well. I had just started lambing here when it happened. I think my movements are accounted for over that time."

"Do you also know a William Birtwhistle?"

"I know a Billy Birtwhistle, yes, again, not well. He was another farmer we did some work for. I helped him out dipping sheep. I was loaned to him when I did a stint on the hill farm belonging to the college. Actually, Eddie was with me that day. It was there he tried to cause me to have an accident. If it hadn't been for Billy's brother I would have fallen in the sheep dip. Eddie had been there before, and was friendly with the daughter I think. He seemed to know his way around. Eddie managed to kill a ewe while we were there. He tried to say it was my fault, but Billy wouldn't have any of it. I had been talking to old Mr Birtwhistle while he was doing whatever he did. Nice old chap. He liked my dog, Drift. What have they to do with all this?"

"Billy Birtwhistle died a few weeks back. At first we thought it was a suicide but forensics have indicated he was murdered. You knew all three of them."

"And I am a common denominator, which makes me as suspect. Whatever I say to you now, will make you more suspicious of me. Even so, I think I need to tell you something I heard. I don't know how true it is, but I will tell you anyway. The problem is you will think I am trying to cast suspicion elsewhere and away from myself."

"Tell me, please."

"I said Eddie knew the daughter. I heard, on the grape vine, that he was selling her drugs. She was on a course at the college at the start of the year but dropped out. The old man told me. I think it was horticulture. I don't remember her from college. I believe she was friendly with Zoe who was on the same course, that was Eddie's girlfriend. It was ages ago when I went to Billy's farm. And I have no idea what happened after that, I think I saw her in the bar with Zoe one evening at a disco, I may have been mistaken."

"Do you know where we can find Zoe?"

"She should be at college."

"Well, she seems to have disappeared, could she be with Eddie do you think?"

"I very much doubt it, she is scared to death of him, hates him."

"What do you know about railways?"

"Trains run on them."

Saul allowed a flash of temper to escape him.

"Don't be flippant with me, madam! Have you ever had anything to do with railways in any way?"

"Yes, and no. I have dealt with incidents on the railway lines, and travelled by train quite a bit, but nothing more."

"In what capacity have you dealt with incidents?"

"When I was in the police."

"Did you retire early?"

"I had been ill, and came out on a medical pension. I don't see that any of that is relevant to what I am here for today."

"Why be so defensive about it?"

"I'm not, by all means find out, you will anyway."

She looked up at Saul and stared him out. It was a trick he used himself and he was surprised and rather annoyed that she was better at it than he was. She was so in control of the interview, he found himself becoming very uneasy. He needed to rattle her a bit, but didn't know how. There was something nagging at him, that he had missed something important, but he couldn't think what it was. He decided to do a bit of fishing.

"Did you ever have a relationship with Mike Grady?"

There was a pause and then she replied calmly, "No, never, nor would I have wanted to."

"Did you have one with Eddie Sullivan?"

This time he got through to her and she showed a momentary sign of annoyance. She glared at him and said, in an over-controlled voice, "Please, whatever you may think of me, credit me with taste, if nothing else. No, I did not, I find him quite repellent."

"Did you always?"

"No, not at first. I did try to befriend him, at the start of the course, but I soon found I despised him. I cooled off, and he didn't like it. I saw, sooner than the others, that he was a very unpleasant chap, and tried to keep as much distance as I could, whilst remaining civil. Several things happened to make me realize what an unspeakable shit he is. Mike tried to persuade me that I had misjudged him and not to be so critical. He said it would make the course run easier if I was a bit more friendly."

"What did you do?"

"I became civil, and utterly correct but refused to cover for the mistakes Eddie made. We all make mistakes, and cover for each other, but Eddie never did, instead he would try to shift the blame for his howlers on anyone but himself. He did it to Steve, Alison, Haggis, Amy and Janet. One of the students had her car wrecked one night. The blame was put on poor Steve, but it was Eddie who came forward and said it was Steve. Steve told me he was innocent but couldn't prove it. I believed him."

"How do you know it was Eddie? You do, don't you?"

"I just do. I was told in confidence, and will not say."

"How unwise of you. Please reconsider. Who was Mike seeing, what is her name?"

"A woman called Collette, from the Equine staff. It isn't common knowledge, I just know."

"How?"

"I get up early. I don't sleep well. I was always the first up and off to walk my dog and sometimes it was really early and I would walk through the woods to the far meadow and sometimes even further and come back past the few houses about a mile down the road. There is a way. There is a footpath that leads behind the Lucky Horseshoe B&B not far from the college. I saw them together in one of the rooms. I saw them twice, as I was walking back on the second occasion, Mike passed me in his car, and clocked me. Not long after she passed in her car, a blue Toyota. Later that day he asked me where I had been, I said out walking, and he asked me if I had seen anyone I knew on the walk. I said I hadn't. He knew, that I knew, I think, but could hardly ask me directly. It was none of my business. I do notice things."

"Surely, to get there from the far meadows beyond the woods, you would have to cross the railway line?"

"Yes, true, there is a way across. I found it by accident when Drift chased a rabbit in there. I haven't advertised it. It isn't an official crossing and technically I expect I was breaking the rules by using it."

"Tell me where it is."

"That meadow, it is called Pump House field, has a ditch beside the railway embankment. Behind a large clump of brambles and docks and a bit of meadow sweet, is a culvert that runs under the line. It is not large but by stooping I could get through. It is quite close to the emergency signal phone where the trains pause sometimes. It comes out in a rough patch and then onto a footpath. The only other person who knows about it is Nick the shepherd. He warned me not to get caught using it. I rather like Nick. We have had our differences, but he is a good shepherd and I have learned a lot from him."

"What did Nick think of Mike Grady?"

"I think you had better ask him."

"I am asking you. You must have some idea."

"Not much, I suspect, Nick tends to run with the hare and hunt with the hounds, and can be a bit two-faced, but can also be very kind, and understanding. He has a difficult role to maintain. I would not presume to make any judgement on his attitude towards Mike."

"But you know, I'm sure of it. As you said, you notice things. I wish you would be up front with me. You are only telling me what you want me to know, and carefully avoiding telling me other things that might be very helpful to me."

"Am I? What exactly do you want me to say? We both know I am a suspect and if I were not quite a prominent one, you, at your rank, would not be wasting your time with me. You would like to trip me up, unsettle me with questions and by putting me under pressure to say something I might later regret. I know how to do it, I have used it myself. I am quite prepared to help you, but on my terms. I have no wish to put my neck into a noose of your making. I happen to be innocent as you will find out in due course, if you are half as bright as I think you are. I am not the only common denominator, I'm sure. Whilst it would give me great gratification to have an apology from Grady, for the injustices he has done, I would hardly obtain that by knocking him off now. Will you be wanting a DNA sample and fingerprints from me?"

"Yes. Are you prepared to give them?"

"Willingly. What else do you want to talk about?"

"Is there anything else you consider relevant?"

"Not really, no. Next time you want to talk to me, ask me to come in of my own accord, which I will do, or have the evidence to arrest me. That way I would at least get a meal. I'm starving. I am also diabetic. I need to eat. I want to go back and finish my work not to mention feeding my dog."

"Do you have and are you willing to surrender a passport?"

"Yes to both those. Can I talk to you off the record?"

"Why?"

"I need to tell you something important, not about this murder, but something else. I would like your advice."

"Would you rather talk to DI Allenby here?"

"No, I would rather talk to you. I am sure you are very nice, ma'am, but I think Mr Catchpole is the one I need to talk to."

"All right. Celia, I think we had better get Miss Green something to eat, and do you need insulin?"

"Yes, it was in my jacket pocket. Could I have my jacket back please? The insulin is in the tin. I am sure you have already checked it."

"Would fish and chips do you? There is a chippy round the corner."

"I have no money, you will have to pay, until I can pay you back when I get back to the farm."

"It's all right, I will stand you this so long as you are straight with me and not wasting my time. Deal?"

"Deal."

Within minutes they were in a more comfortable and more relaxing room and her items of property were returned to her. Diana made a point of safely disposing of the soiled syringe and then took out the tin from her pocket. When Celia left the room, Saul said, "Why did you leave the job, Diana?"

"There were several reasons, but the main one was my diabetes. It is only type two but at the moment, long hours, and the stress of what has been going on at college have not helped. They offered me a nine-to-five job, to keep me in the force but I didn't want that. I will be honest with you, I had a bit of a problem with a senior officer who was rather like Grady, and the end result is I do not trust senior officers much, but I think you might be a bit different, at least I hope you are. By all means find out why I left, and the circumstances of it. You will anyway. Now what else did you want to know?"

"I am interested in the rank you held in the force."

"Why?"

"Just interested. Who told you about Eddie stitching up Steve?"

"Nick. I'm not sure if he knew or just suspected. I can also tell you that he hated Mike's guts. Mike was trying to get him the sack. Nick found out about some money missing from the sheep budget, quite a lot of money. He had reason to think Mike had pocketed it. Nick asked my advice, he put it in the form of a hypothetical question, but I knew. I never made a secret of what I had done before. It was also Nick who told me that Eddie was selling drugs especially to Billy's daughter, if you say I told you I shall deny it."

"Very well. What is it that you are so worried about, and that you don't want my woman colleague to hear? I don't think you like her much, do you?"

"It isn't that I don't like her, I am sure she is a good person, but she isn't that bright you know, academically, maybe, but she hasn't got very good people skills. Intuition isn't her strong point. She will rise in the ranks but it will not be as a practical copper, it will be a rather academic path. I can't identify with that. You, however, understand people. I have a problem. You intimated that all these three deaths are connected. I know why you suspect me, but please consider that Eddie is a stronger common denominator, along with a few others. When I found out this morning that Eddie was nearby, I wondered why. If he is the killer, and I suspect he may well be, then something has happened to make him flip. If he has lost the plot, then I might just be the next on his list. He really hates me. You think you haven't rattled me, don't you? Well, you have, not so much by trying to do so, but by what you have told me. Things are starting to slot horribly into place, and I don't like the way they are going. I may well have an overactive imagination, but I am scared, very scared. I would not presume to tell you your job, and I am sure you are very good at it, but I think I may be in considerable danger. If you could trust me enough to tell me more, I might be able to fill in a few gaps for you, but while I am still a suspect you can't and I know it. Now what do I do?"

"I do see your problem. I could hold you in custody, but not for long. If I did, how would you take it?"

"It isn't practicable. I have work to do and a dog to look after. I will not leave Jim in the lurch. If I don't go back to the farm, I will fail my course and all my efforts will be for nothing, I cannot afford to miss the next bit, when we learn to shear, and I need to know how to do that. In college I have been watching my back against them, Mike and Eddie, I mean, for some time. I think you will find that in more ways than one they are very alike. Just at the moment the farm is where I will be safest. Do you see my dilemma?"

"Yes I do, and I think you see mine."

"Yes, which is why I wanted to talk to you alone, so you could keep it to yourself until you make a decision. If you need me to act as bait for Eddie I will, but you need to understand. Of course, I might be the murderer just waiting for a chance to knock him off too, I see how it might look."

"And if he is the killer, he might be setting you up to take the fall for the murders. If we take you back to the farm how could you keep yourself safe there if he did turn up?"

"I have a couple of aces up my sleeve. My dog hates him, so does his. First of all, Jim is a staunch ally. I have told him a lot of this already. He would look out for me if he knew there was danger. The second ace is that in the month I have been there I have got to know the place. There is a hidden cave in the woods, near the field you found me in. And this cave has an escape route that not even Jim knows about. Jim doesn't like caves but I have enjoyed the sport of potholing for years. I could give anyone the slip in there, I know a couple of secret ways out, and could take to the hills, provided I had food and insulin, which is already there, I put it there this morning after I got that call about Eddie. Drift will warn me of any strangers present, and has a couple of times before which is how I have avoided two potential non-accidents in the past. I may be way off track but I don't think so. Incidentally, did you know that Mike had a bitter dispute with a neighbour of his? The house he lives in was the subject of a land dispute between him and a neighbouring farmer, and they are still bitter enemies. The other shepherd told me all about it."

"Interesting. You do seem to amass a lot of information. I need to think this through. Can I have your clothes for forensic examination?"

"Now? Don't you think I might get a bit cold without them? Anyway I need that jacket, it is the only weatherproof one I have."

She was laughing at him, and his dislike of her faded.

"If I find you another jacket, can you let my officer have them when you get back to the farm? It is really to eliminate you and to confirm what you have told me."

"I am a size twelve. I do need my tools and phone and things back. Especially the phone in case I need it urgently to summon help."

"Celia has already checked all your things. You knew she had. I will give you an attack alarm to carry. I need to bring Eddie in, and if he turns up, will you set it off?"

"Too right I will, even if I see him from a distance, you haven't met him yet, have you?"

"No."

"I know some of us smell none too good at lambing, but have some air spray ready! I don't think he has washed in months, not since he split up from Zoe. If he has it is to hide something."

"Thanks. Ah, here is your food and you should eat, you have gone very pale. Thank you for trusting me. Here is my card, and I have written on the back of it my personal number in case you need me. Just be careful."

After she had eaten the food and given DNA and fingerprints, Celia drove her back to the farm where Jim was waiting anxiously with Donald. Diana changed her clothes and looked at the jacket she had been given and laughed.

"It will do fine, thanks. Best police issue. You have my number? Here is my passport. Thanks for the grub. I expect we will meet again."

As Celia drove off, Diana watched the car disappearing and then headed for the bathroom and had a hot and much-needed shower.

When Celia got back, she found Saul deep in thought. She said, "Well, I don't know what she told you, but she was trying to bamboozle you. I trust you didn't believe her?"

"She told me exactly what she wanted to and no more. That is a very clever woman, and what is worrying me is I know I have missed something. Several things, I think. I will take the tape and listen to it again. Does anything occur to you?"

"Yes. I think she is guilty. I don't understand why you let her go."

"The little matter of insufficient evidence? No, there is more to her than meets the eye. I just wish I could work it out. I'll see you tomorrow. It is time we all had a break. Goodnight."

Chapter Four

When he finally got into his digs that evening, Saul was pretty exhausted, but made a point of chatting with Eileen and Tom, and learned a lot about what was going on at the college. He rang his wife, and then headed to bed. It had been a very long day, but he couldn't sleep. His interview with Diana was haunting him. He could not identify what he had missed, but knew it was important. There was something about her and the controlled way she had behaved in the interview that worried him. He considered anyone that bright could well be a clever killer but it didn't seem to fit. He was still thinking about it when he went to sleep. During the night he woke suddenly from a nightmare, something that seldom worried him. He had dreamed about the two zero's made of paper on the table. It must have meant something. She had not fiddled with or touched anything else all the time she had been with them. One or two things she had said did not seem at all relevant to what he was investigating, and that worried him too. He decided he needed to know more about her, and determined to do that first thing the next morning.

He arrived at the office at the college about half past six and as he went in, Sandra Lancashire handed him a cup of coffee, and said, "Good morning, sir. DI Allenby left this for you, and I've sorted all the statements we got yesterday. I took over from the night man, I think his name is Bert, at six this morning. He warned me you would be the first one in. I have some messages for you as well but I have not read them yet. Oh, and the train driver says he has remembered something else, and one of the passengers on the train wants to talk to us. Do you want me to go and see them?"

"Let's go together shall we? We can take my car. I need to pick your brains about farming things. Someone will be in soon so we can hand over to them and head off early. Are you being looked after by the others on the squad?"

"Not half, sir. They are a very diverse lot, and get on so well. It isn't quite what I expected, in that it seems so relaxed and everyone knows what they are doing, like they need little or no supervision. It only seems to be the admin side that the skippers handle, as well as the detecting side. I am learning lots. Who is the cartoonist in the squad? They are very good!"

Saul drained his mug and groaned. "Oh no, have they started already? Listen, Sandra, the whole squad seem to produce them. At the end of each case I put them all in a file and keep them. What are they about?"

"I think the best one is about the choice of DI Allenby's footwear in the hills. It depicts her coming into the office leaving pin point muddy tracks all over the floor from her high heels. There is another one, rather a different style, showing a Miss Strongest Woman winner cowping over a sheep and the men around her struggling to pick up a lamb. I found that rather apt."

Saul looked at her in a suspicious way and said, "Do you draw cartoons by any chance?"

"It has been known, yes, sir. You could stop it, why don't you?"

"OK, I'll tell you. It is a very healthy outlet. In this part of the job, as well as in basic coppering, we come across horrid, shocking, evil and disgusting things. We have to stay rational and calm about them even if we are frightened or revolted. The cartoons provide a light-hearted jibe at what we do and they actually help with team work. I expect someone will tell you, if they haven't already that I draw too, and have even been known to contribute occasionally. Very few are aimed at me, I think because of my rank, but I am not sure, they probably hide those from me. If we can't laugh at ourselves then we cannot do our job without falling apart. What is cowping?"

"Tipping or turning a sheep over to trim its feet or bum or to clip it. That's shearing, by the way."

"So you would cowp it over to dag it?"

"That's right, sir, oh here comes Tarik, shall we go? I have statement forms and all that. Geoff kitted me out with an 'enquiry pack' yesterday, and says everyone has one. I replenished mine yesterday, you know exhibit labels, statement forms, cards, victim support leaflets and crime reports and all that. Do I need anything else?"

As Saul drove them into the outskirts of Skipton, he considered he had made a very wise choice selecting Sandra to come on the squad. Once again, he looked into the future and saw her doing his job. They parked in the street and knocked on Neil's door and were let in immediately.

"Thanks for coming, I know this sounds very trivial, but the officer said yesterday if anything occurred to me, however small, I should tell you. When I went down to check if the chap was alive, I thought I heard something, there was a sort of squelchy noise and then a faint soft rushing sound, like wind in the grass, except there was no wind that I could feel. There was a strange smell too, and I can't place it. Then John came down and all I could smell after that was his vomit. I felt a bit sick myself so it might be my imagination. There were several smells, but one was sort of salty, I presume that was the blood, and then an unwashed, shitty smell but I noticed the chap had messed himself from the state of the trousers, they were wet, but then there was this sort of sweet rather pleasant smell. I wondered if it was the meadowsweet that grows there but it isn't in flower this time of year."

"If you can identify any of these smells, would you let us know? You were not the only one to smell something. Did you see anyone as the train approached?"

"No, not that day. I often see some of the students, but not recently. The most regular one is a woman, not as young as the others, with a large collie with a very white face. That is the one who is there earlier than the others. If the train is late then there are other students with their dogs. I haven't seen any for the last couple of weeks."

Saul and Sandra called next at the Ambulance station where Donna made them a cup of tea and said, "I was going to call in at the Police station today, but I thought it might be important. I was on that train, I am most mornings. We often have to stop there and wait. That morning, me and another chap, Aiden, saw the driver get out, and then go down the bank. Then the guard went down, and it was then I got up to put a sweet wrapper in the bin behind the seat near me. I looked out of the other side of the train. Down the embankment is a rough bit of land, and then I think a path between some of the fields. There is a wall, a stone one. As the train was pulling away, I saw a man there, and he hadn't come down the path or from anywhere else that I could see. He was just under the embankment walking away from it, towards the wall. I never saw his face but he looked like a farmer and he was hurrying, but not running, and he jumped over the wall and then he must have hidden behind it. It is only a low wall and I would have seen if he had walked off. I watched until the train pulled away, but he never reappeared."

"Can you describe him?"

"Sort of, green jacket, like what farmer's wear, wellies I think, they looked wet or very shiny. He had a cloth cap on, a sort of grey tweedy one, and I have seen him there before, often with several dogs, on the other side of the line in the college field where the students go with their sheep dogs. I don't know if Aiden saw him but at the time we didn't know what had happened and thought nothing of it."

"Would you know this man again?"

"I might."

"Did he have his dog with him?"

"I didn't see no dog."

Saul and Sandra managed to find Aiden at his work. He said, "Yes, I did see a man in that rough bit. Donna was watching him and I glanced up to see what she was looking at. I paid little attention to him. I remember thinking it were a bit early for a country walk, like."

By the time Saul and Sandra got back to the office the rest of the team were in, and were heading off to do their allotted enquiries. They had a brief meeting and one officer said, "We managed to find all but three of the students on that course. I interviewed the Canadian girl, Alison Stanovitch. She was at the college and her boyfriend was with her, together in her room for the whole night so they say. The wardens were most helpful, and confirmed that there were two in there at some point. In the morning Alison and her boyfriend were up early and had gone to the computer room, and were there from about six to nine and the computer logs confirm it. They had also been there the previous evening from six till about one, finishing some sort of assignment."

"Then we went and found Ruth Parker, in a caravan about ten miles away on a site. She had been working a few days at some gardens since she got back from her lambing attachment and says she was babysitting for some friends of hers and stopped overnight at their place. She and Alison had some pretty scathing things to say about the college, and both admitted they hated Grady."

"Thank you, Paul. Julie, what did you find out?"

"I spoke to Alex who lives on a big farm not far away. He was there with his family and so was the fellow student, David Long, who is from the Cotswolds. They went down the local pub the evening before and the father said the two of them got in about midnight, steaming drunk and he packed them off to bed. He wasn't pleased about it. Then we went on to see the young lass, Amy. She had been with her family all evening, and was up early helping with the milking the next morning. She was very distressed about Grady's death. Her mother

80

explained she has led a very sheltered life and it was a great shock to the girl."

"So far so good. Did we find the Irish lad, Steve? Or the Scots lad, Haggis, Peter is it?"

"Steve is still over in Ireland flying back the day after tomorrow and has been there for a week. I got the Garda to check. The Scottish lad has been at his family farm in the highlands of Scotland for a week or more."

"Who saw the woman, Janet? Was that you, Sandra?"

"Yes, I went with Geoff. She was up all night, with the shepherd at the farm she is attached to and they had a busy night and can be accounted for. They had to call out the vet about one a.m., I also took an interesting statement from the farm secretary here, Rachel Colebrook, who gave us lots of details and addresses and things. Very helpful."

"Thank you, well, Celia and I found the woman, Diana Green, and took her into the nick and interviewed her there. She was very interesting and I have not yet made my mind up about her. May I ask that if she contacts us I am told immediately. It could be important. You strongly suspect her don't you, Celia? Anyway, I have circulated the details of the other student, Eddie Sullivan, who we know is a disqualified driver, deals drugs and is a violent person. We looked for him but can't find him. His car has gone from the car park here, but apparently is unlikely to get far due to its condition. I want to know the moment he is spotted too. How did you get on with Nick the shepherd, Darren?"

"Not very well at all. He was not forthcoming. He admits loathing Grady, had little good to say about Sullivan, and told me very firmly we are barking up the wrong tree with Green,

I almost got the feeling he was warning me off about suspecting her or even getting involved with her. His wife and family are away at the moment and has no alibi and says he was at home until he went out to see the duty students in at six in the morning. He took the bale off the baler the night before and it is in a pen in the sheep shed. He left the tractor in the barn and hung up the keys on the hook in the office where they are kept. I think he needs seeing again."

"Has Zoe turned up yet?"

"No and she is missing. Her friends are quite worried, nor do her parents know where she is. I got the warden to check her room and her purse, phone and keys are still there. The room looks a bit of a mess, but that is not uncommon according to the warden. Her friends say she is meticulous about keeping the room tidy and never goes anywhere without the phone."

"From what I have learned, mainly from Green but it is backed up by other sources, we have now established several links between the three deaths and it all centres on this college. We need to do some re-interviewing, as I suspect we have not been told anything like the whole truth. Celia is allotting tasks today, and I will need her to find Collette from Equine studies who was Grady's lover, and Darren, could you see what her husband knows about. How did you get on with the widow, Kate?"

"Much as you would expect. She knew he was having an affair and didn't care who with. She is mildly upset but not as bad as I would expect. The step daughter was a bit tearful but she and her step father had been rowing for weeks, mainly over her new boyfriend that Grady hated. She won't say who it is and the mother says she only knows it is a student from the college here."

"How long has she been seeing this lad, do we know?"

"I do. I went with Kate. I got to talk to the girl while Kate was talking to the mother. She wouldn't say who it was, but she has been seeing him for a couple of months and then she asked for my help. She thinks she is pregnant by him, and said Grady suspected as much. She didn't dare tell him who it was, because she knew he didn't like him. I have arranged to go with her to the doctors this evening, I said I would have to clear it with you, sir, I hope I have done the right thing?"

"Well done, Sandra, yes you have. Is there something else?"

"I don't think she was that upset by Grady's death. I think she was just scared at being pregnant. If her mother had not been there I think she would have said more. She says she wants to talk this evening."

"How old is she?"

"Sixteen, sir, she said that Grady confiscated her mobile phone last weekend because he was trying to stop her seeing her boyfriend. She said Grady was a control freak. That girl is scared, sir. I gave her my mobile number in case she is inclined to tell me more."

"We had better not crowd her then, get as much as you can from her and then help she needs if you can."

"She said the whole family are Catholic and divorce and abortion are not options."

"The plot thickens, Celia, what was your impression of Diana Green yesterday?"

"She was very much in control of what she said yesterday. There are many things she is not telling us, not because she doesn't know but thinks we don't need to. Unless she came clean with you. It was not the whole truth and I felt she was manipulating the pair of us."

"Yes, I know I found it quite unnerving. She used most of the interview techniques on me that I use on others. If she is being straight, I think she may be in danger from this Sullivan chap, or he from her. Quite frightening. I never did find out why she started to dislike this Eddie."

"I think I know, sir, Janet told me. She and Diana are friends, good ones. She says Diana is very generous and supportive to the rest of the course and has done most of them many favours helped them in some way or other. She helped Janet get a new car after someone wrecked hers. Janet didn't think it was Steve. Eddie begged Diana to lend him some money when the course started said he was waiting for funds to come over from Ireland. He never paid her a penny back and laughingly said she shouldn't have been so stupid to give it to him in the first place and he would tell anyone it was a gift. He did the same to a couple of others too and Diana found out about it. One of them was Haggis, Diana got him out of a jam that Eddie had got him in. When Janet spoke to Diana about it, she said Diana said it was bought experience and she wouldn't push it further on her own behalf, didn't want to advertise her stupidity. Janet believed it was Eddie who had wrecked her car because she had tried to tell him to pay back the others who had loaned him money."

Saul went down to the sheep pens with Darren. Nick was rounding up what seemed to be a huge flock of massive sheep when they arrived. Saul watched in admiration and a dawning respect as Nick directed the dogs, and there were three of them, as the sheep meekly passed through the gate into a large pen. Nick called to Saul to close the gate on them, which he did, and then came over and said, "You must be the big boss. I've been expecting you. We need to talk. Not here. I'll just put the dogs away and then I will meet you, and just you, down there. I think I could do with a walk, a private one with you."

Somewhat intrigued, Saul waited for Nick while Darren moved away. Nick joined him and said, "This way, I don't want to be overheard, and trees have ears round here. It is a fine day, follow me."

Beside the fence of a large field with no other tracks, woods or trees nearby, they sat on a fallen oak tree and Nick said, "I rang Diana last night. I have been worried about her. I actually think quite a lot of her. We have had our disagreements but I think a great deal of her. She is about the brainiest person I have ever met. Now we jog along fine, but I don't know why she wants to be a shepherd. You never need to show her anything more than once, the hill shepherd says the same. I gave her a glowing report for her last practical and the one before, so did he. Then I spoke to Rachel who tore me up for arse paper for failing her. She said she would have a go at the hill shepherd for doing the same. Neither of us failed her, we both gave her distinctions. For a start, her dog is better trained and a better worker than any of mine and that is saying something, Janet is pretty good too and she got marked right down and it could only have been by Grady. I'm glad he's dead. He had not only re-written my reports and incidentally put a load of spelling mistakes and grammatical errors in them, he had forged both of our signatures on them. I took it to the principal last week and when I spoke to Diana yesterday, she told me Grady had been doing it to all the girls all the time. No, I am wrong, not to Ruth, mainly because she is pretty crap anyway. He doesn't need to mark her down. I arranged a Sheep dog trial, one of my friends set it up for me, for the students and I asked him to judge it and assess all of them. He gave Janet top marks and Diana one less, ninety-eight percent and ninety-seven percent. I found his report had been doctored too. Eddie's had always been marked up from fail to credit at least but he shouldn't even be here and no way should he ever be allowed to work with animals. I told Grady I was taking the whole thing to the principal. We had a massive row about it and he stormed off. Anyway, one of the things I need to tell you is that Diana isn't half as tough as she makes out. She was pretty close to cracking before she went off on lambing attachments. Both the farmers where she has been have told me how brilliant she is and how she works practically every hour under the sun, moon, fog, whatever. Sure she is always reasoned, sometimes totally inflexible, but one of the kindest people I know. She has the patience of a saint, especially with small animals. She listens hard, I'll give her that. When I spoke to her yesterday she asked me to talk to you and tell you what I think of Grady. I have, right?"

"Definitely you have. Anything else?"

"Yes. I knew that Eddie tried to grass up young Steve over Janet's car. Like Bobby Birtwhistle's lass is on drugs, got from Eddie. Like Mike's stepdaughter has been going out with Eddie recently. Like it was me that grassed Eddie up over his driving his car, to the cops. She knew I had, but never said a dicky bird. It was Janet that told me Eddie owed Diana five hundred pounds. Lots of things."

"Why did you not admit to Eddie it was you?"

"I didn't want a nasty accident, and Di told me not to. Every time anyone falls out with his Irish obnoxiousness, nasty things happen to them. He even boasts about it. Haggis upset him, and next morning Haggis was under the silo when the chute stuck open and he could have been killed. He was buried but Amy pulled him out. Eddie had been down there late the evening before. I made him shovel all the spilt feed into bags 'cos I knew it was him. That night all my car tyres were punctured. He hates Di, with a vengeance because she stands up to him."

"Did you not report all this to someone?"

"Of course I did. Grady. He assured me it was being dealt with. Like hell it was! The principal, the old one, not Hardaker, knew nothing about it. Something happened, and Eddie became a bit wary of Di. She begged me not to tell anyone, but I think I need to tell you and break her confidence."

"So do I!"

"She and Eddie were working in the sheep shed one evening. He lost his temper with a ewe, I think he had had a drink or two, which isn't allowed. Neither of them knew I was there. She pulled him off, and told him she wouldn't stand for it, and told him what she thought of him. It was wonderful, not a swear word but some splendid descriptions. She told him to get out of the shed, she would finish up. I was going over to break it up, but before I could, he had drawn a huge hunting knife on her, from his boot and was advancing on her. I was about to rush over and help her but before I could she had not only disarmed him and put him on the ground, none too gently I might add, but she had sprained his wrist in the process, possibly because he resisted. She put him in an arm lock, and literally kicked him out of the building. I followed him back to the block and then went back to check on her. She was still pretty angry. She gave me the knife, explained, very accurately what had happened, and I never let on I had seen it, and she and I patched up the ewe and she nursed it back to health over the next few days. I put the knife in my office drawer, locked it and was going to hand it in to the principal but the next day it had gone and the drawer lock was forced and broken."

"Do you know of a hidden way under the railway line from Pump House field?"

"Sure I do. So does Diana. I warned her not to get caught using it. Someone else knows about it too. I haven't been in there recently, but half way along there is a hollow behind a brick. Someone uses it to hide things in, because often it has been used. I asked Di if it was her but she said no, but she had noticed it. She doesn't miss a trick. I also found an empty metal box in it not long ago. I took it out and put it in the waste bin, but the next day I thought I saw Eddie with it or one very like it. Mind you, it is a common type of box. Most students keep tools in such boxes."

"Do you know where Eddie is?"

"No, gone off in that car of his I think."

"Is his dog still here?"

"Yes, but that means nothing. He doesn't care for or about that poor dog, so the rest of us are looking after it. Di asked me to try and buy it for her, on the quiet. It has potential. I think it didn't help that the dog loved Di, all the dogs do, even mine, who I thought were one-man dogs. She can work any dog, it is a rare talent."

"Who do you think killed Grady?"

"I think the list of those who didn't want to would be shorter. I would have said that Di wasn't capable until I saw how she handled Eddie that day. I think it was Eddie."

"You also had a motive. Did you kill him?"

"True, but I am a coward, a wimp. The thought is nice, but no, I didn't. If I had I would tell you. I'd probably be boasting about it by now. How was he killed by the way?"

"You don't want to know the details. Not a nice way."

"Oh, good. No it wasn't me. It wasn't Di either. I am sure of that. Have you done with me? I must get these sheep dosed. Some students will be down to help me in a few minutes."

Nick got up and strode off back to the sheep sheds. Darren who had been watching from a distance joined Saul and said,

"How did it go, sir?"

Saul, standing up from the tree trunk, brushed himself down and smiled wryly and said, "Well, that told me!"

Together they walked back to their office as Saul chuckled softly to himself.

Chapter Five

As Saul walked back into the office in the wing of the College, he passed the police technical services guy, who gave him a cheery greeting.

"It is all set up, guv, I've put a couple of secure lines in, and changed a few locks on doors, here is your office key. They have a safe in there and have found the keys, so here is your safe key. It's a long time since I was here, but years ago I did a course here. You know there is a toilet block, shower room and cloakroom at the end of this corridor? I've checked everything works. You know my son is on a course here? He is training to be a landscape gardener. He was telling me about this murder thing. He knows some of the courses this chap Grady was teaching. Says one of the lads is a right shit. He says he saw him yesterday, with a lass he thought had thrown this lad over, she was in this boy's car. The girl didn't look very happy."

"Well, thanks for what you have done, Ivan. Your son didn't mention any names did he?"

"I can't remember them; do you want me to ask him? I can ring him now if you like? He's at home today. I think he is a bit sweet on the lass, Zoe I think her name is, and oh yes, the boy's name is Eddie? My lad don't like him at all. I'll give him a ring now, before he leaves for football. I'll come and tell you. Is that OK?"

"Ivan, you are truly an angel from heaven! Check with your lad, Jeremy isn't it? If you would, and come back to me."

"Well, fancy you remembering my lad's name, sir. I don't remember you meeting him?

"Yes you do, a few years back at the Christmas party for the kids. He got a football kit and a light sabre, if I remember right. Good-looking lad, tall for his age, good manners."

"He'll be chuffed you remember him, you've been one of his heroes for ages now."

"What, along with the whole Manchester United squad? How flattering!"

As Ivan scurried off down the corridor Saul blessed his memory for details. It helped a lot sometimes. He found it very helpful to keep in with the technical crew. He dashed into his office and put several calls through and a couple to the Garda in Ireland. Geoff, his sergeant came in and Saul waved him into a nearby seat and when the call had finished, turned to Geoff and said, "Right, what can you tell me?"

"Ivan said it is Zoe and Eddie. Look, Zoe is definitely missing. Her mother is frantic. I've set up a missing person enquiry, running it as part of Operation Cain. That lass Sandra is a very bright spark, we can use her, and she is young enough to relate to all these students. They make me feel very old sometimes. Look, sir, I have been listening to what is being said, and I have a bad feeling about this Eddie. We searched his room just now, the college let us in and gave us permission, don't worry I got it written down. It is a veritable pig sty. I've put out an 'all ports warning' on him too. In his room we found several passports so I suspect he is using another one, he seems to have quite a few aliases."

"Good man, I had forensics on just now. They have identified a drug in Grady's blood that was present in the other two bodies. They are sending details through, it isn't Rohypnol but something similar that paralyses the physical body but keeps the mind alert. Never heard of it before. We have a serial killer on our hands, Geoff. One who has lost the plot completely, and who is both cruel and dangerous. Will you call the dog section and get them to search for Eddie where he was last seen which is near the village of Hebden? I think Celia has the exact details. She got them from Diana Green when she drove her back to the farm. We need to find both Sullivan or whatever he is called and this lass Zoe."

"Leave it with me, sir, I'll get all that in motion, and I will start making enquiries in the drink outlets, because from the state of his room he is a heavy drinker, a very heavy one but…"

"Yes, Southern Comfort I believe? I thought so. What is troubling you? Spit it out."

"Yes you always know. It is this Green woman, DI Allenby is convinced she is the murderer, and says you can't see it. That she doesn't like this Green woman is very obvious. Do you know why she feels like that?"

"I think so, yes. Diana Green very quickly and very accurately assessed Celia's character within an hour of meeting her. She is more than a match for Celia and I am afraid that I may have met my match in her too. She may well be the killer but I don't think so. These murders are far too clumsy for it to be this woman, she knows far too much and quite frankly scares me to death. I get the feeling she is running rings round me but she is also giving me clues and I can't work them out. I need to talk to her again. What I have just found out, or rather what I have not found out and should have been able to, means I need to know some important things. I am going to see her again, now. In the meantime, I need to know if we have any birth certificate for Sullivan and I need to know who his father is, if known. I tried to find out a bit about Green just now, about her police service with Wiltshire. They confirmed she is an ex-officer and of a very high rank, but wouldn't tell me what, and she is now a police pensioner because of her diabetes, but wouldn't tell me what work she was involved in, and then, and very politely and firmly, told that I didn't need to know it, and my security clearance is not high enough, and intimated that I should leave her alone."

"What! I thought you had the highest security you can get?"

"So did I. It looks like today is the day I get put firmly in my place. However, that aside, try to get Celia to leave off telling everyone it is Green, and I want protection for Grady's wife, stepdaughter and as for Nick the shepherd here, I want him watched, covertly. I want all the firearms users on the squad to draw weapons and everyone to be very careful. I am going to draw a firearm and then I want Toby and Sanjit to join me, with guns, and I am going back up to Moorside Farm. I am just going to ring to find out where she is, from Jim the farmer. Incidentally, can you thank the joker who has put sheep loo roll in the toilets? It gave me about the first smile of the day."

Geoff Bickerstaff was a competent and effective Detective Sergeant who had been on the murder squad for some time. He soon had things under way and when Saul walked in the main office a few minutes later it was a scene of feverish activity. Saul held his hand up and everyone stopped what they were doing and listened.

"Things have got worse. I can get no reply from Diana Green's phone, and I spoke to the farmer, Jim Gardiner, and he can't find her, not since this morning. He has been looking. He was just about to ring us to raise the alarm. Geoff, Celia, arrange back up and as many troops as you can. I have a very bad feeling about this."

*

The old mine was cold and damp and very dark. The only light was from a candle on the ground, well beyond Zoe's reach. She had come to in the dark, terrified. Eddie had arrived after what seemed hours, and loosened her bonds a bit, and left her food before locking her back in the cage. He had left her blankets and a sleeping bag but no clothes. He had laughed when she had begged him to leave the candle and had sneeringly found a short candle stub that wouldn't last long. She had had to pay for the light and was disgusted with herself. Even when she had been going out with him, sex hadn't been much fun, but she had borne it just to have some light. There was a manic manner about him. She knew he was going to kill her eventually. She searched for some escape route but could find nothing. He had chained her to the wall, and she couldn't even reach the mesh of the cage. She could see her clothes and other things a bit further away. Well out of her reach.

She had tried screaming, but all that happened was the eerie echo of her own screams coming back at her. She knew she was in an old mine, because the chamber was obviously man-made. He had told her she could scream all she wanted, that it wouldn't help her as no one would hear. When she tried to reason with him, he hit her. When she began to cry, he had laughed and he was obviously enjoying it. When he had raped her he had hurt her and he had enjoyed that too. He had ripped off her panties and was delighted when he found blood on them. She could see them on the clothes pile. He had boasted that her parents would receive them one day. Even though she was terrified, she was also angry. There was more to Zoe than most people saw. Although her head ached, and she was cold she sat and thought, and looked around her. The candle started to gutter. She wrapped herself up as warmly as she could and overcame the panic that was threatening to engulf her. She began to look for something to pick the locks.

*

As Saul pulled up at Moorside Farm, the armed response units followed him in. Jim and Donald were there and several other men and women he did not know. Jim hastily explained, "We have called all the local farmers and helpers we can find. There are more on the way, shepherds, cowmen, everyone. They all want to help. The phone signal only works in a few places here, but I have kept trying her. I can't find her dog either. I did find her crook, and left it exactly as I found it. I think she meant me to find it and to leave it for you to see. I don't understand it but you being a high-ranking man might be cleverer than me and understand. She left one or two other things there. Shall I show you?"

"Please, is it far? Can your friends that know this area help the other officers? More are coming. We need someone who knows the ground."

"About a mile, here jump on the back of the quad it will be quicker and it is quite a climb. With a gammy leg you might struggle. The others can follow in Jem's Land Rover what is coming now. She told me what she said to you. You are wrong to suspect her, you know."

Saul did not enjoy the quad ride up the hill and hung on desperately until they arrived in a large field with a lot of sheep. On the ground a crook was carefully placed pointing toward a thick wood at the edge of the field not far away. Beside the crook was a set of clipping shears open and stuck into the ground. A bit further on was a syringe with what looked like blood in it. It was almost, but not quite, hidden in a clump of rushes and was also pointing towards the wood. Saul radioed up for a photographer to record everything.

"Jim, do you know any caves in the woods here?"

"No but she has told me there is one there but never showed me. I did hear a car engine earlier and wondered about it, sounded like an old Land Rover. I wondered about it and that's why I started to look for her. I also heard a shot, and I thought it came from these woods."

Saul looked at the crook and began to walk towards the wood. At the fence the undergrowth was fierce and he could see nowhere where it was disturbed. He stood back and thought about it. In the mud, a few feet away was an upright stick with what looked like fresh blood on the top of it. Saul began to be really worried. When he looked there was a small blood spot beside it under a tree branch. There were no signs of anything having moved through the undergrowth. He looked up, and smiled.

"How clever! I think I can see how she did this. Look someone has been in that tree. She knew I would understand. Jim, do us a favour, go back and get the dog unit to come up here please and get the rest of the troops to search this wood. I take it there is a gate somewhere? She has left a trail for me, which means she is in trouble. I am worried by the blood. Was it just one shot you heard?"

"Yes and I wasn't sure about that. I'll bring torches and a rope. She took a rope a few days ago, said she needed to borrow it. I offered her the new nylon one but she said she was happy with the larger thicker hemp one."

Saul looked at the undergrowth and then at the tree. He decided to save his trousers from complete destruction in the brambles and leapt up and grasped the branch above him and pulled himself up. He moved along the branch, carefully until he saw a scuff mark in the lichen on an adjacent tree, and leaning over carefully got into the next tree, and found another mark a bit further on. Wondering if he needed committing, he shuffled along it, thinking how his squad would enjoy watching him, and thankful that they were not and envisaging the cartoons that would follow. Looking down he saw a disturbance in the undergrowth below. Thankfully the brambles had given way to moss. He lowered himself down and made a similar impression and it was at this point he knew he was on the right track. He followed the drops of blood and found an animal track leading into the denser part of the wood.

He found the imprint of a small boot, of a size a woman would wear. He remembered that Diana wore such a set of boots. He looked around and found a dog's paw print, but nothing else. It looked as if the ground had been smoothed out. He heard the others arriving at the edge of the wood. He moved towards a small outcrop by the base of a large tree and found more blood drops. They were congealed but not old.

He followed them over the rocky knoll, an into a small depression and clearing, where the blood drops stopped. Other officers had caught up with him, looking rather dishevelled as they had come through the brambles. He cast around and they spread out, but found nothing. He went back and sat on the rock next to the last blood clot, and thought about it. He tried calling but there was no response. He picked some moss off his trousers and looked down at the moss beneath his feet. It did not look quite right. As he reached down he felt a cold draught on his hand. He moved some moss and then called the others back.

The cave entrance was heavily concealed and rather small. Torches were fetched and someone offered him a set of overalls, which he gratefully put on. He was not keen on tight places, but was not going to wimp out in front of his troops, and followed a young and keen firearms officer into the cave. Soon he could crawl. In his light he could see blood drops on the pale limestone. Gradually the roof came up and he could stand in a narrow passage. There was a small stream running across his wellington boots but they were already filled with cold water from the crawl, and his feet were soaking. They followed the passage but soon it got very low and ended in a pool that the firearms officer informed him was called a sump.

Retracing their steps Saul noticed a small gap near the roof. He helped the young officer up and hauled himself up on a rope that was thrown down for him and then crawled away from the stream passage into a dry, rather muddy area where he could sit up. He looked around and watching him from under an overhanging ledge was a large white-faced dog. He called to it, "Drift, here, girl. It's all right. Good girl."

The dog growled at him and shrank back. They had to wait until Jim arrived and called it out. Tied around the neck of the dog was a handkerchief. Written on the handkerchief, in what looked like blood was 'Under the stone'. They picked up every stone they could see and finally Saul found a plastic bag with a wad of papers inside, obviously torn from a notebook. Jim shone the torch as they read, Sir, thanks for looking. Please look after my dog. Eddie turned up here just before lunch. Drift warned me but I only just had time to leave the crook and things before I had to take off. He has at least one gun and he winged me. I'm not badly hurt and the bleeding has almost stopped. He is trying to find me and I don't have much time. Before he got me I saw him, and he had Zoe in the car with him. Now the bleeding has stopped I can get away. Go out the way you came and use Drift to find my track on the edge of the wood. I am going out another way that I don't think you, or he for that matter, will fit through. It comes out just into the moor. I will try and see where he goes. Don't let Drift off the lead or you may lose her or he might just shoot her and I couldn't bear that. My phone won't work and the attack thing you gave me was hit by the bullet. I was trying to press it when I got hit in the arm. As soon as I can I will ring you. He drove off toward the top of the moor. There may be tracks. It was an old mark 2 Land Rover, British Racing Green.

Once out of the cave Saul let go his exasperation.

"I might have known she would do something daft like this! Now we have to find her, as well as him and Zoe. Why the hell couldn't she just lie low and wait for us in safety? I know, I think she has gone off on some heroic venture to rescue Zoe. Why did she have to be so brave?"

"Sir, I am wondering, do you not think she might just be trained to do this kind of thing? It looks like she more than knows what she is doing. I was in the SAS and I know someone with training when I come across them. Either that or she is the modern version of a female James Bond."

Saul stared at the man in front of him, and suddenly the penny dropped.

"I have been quite blind and I am such a fool. Thank you, officer, I am sorry I don't know your name."

"Callum, sir, Callum Doyle and I am a skipper in the firearms unit. Stationed in Harrogate."

"Well, Callum, I need you to stick with me like glue. I am going to need your help and advice. Come on."

They followed Jim and Drift up over the moor above the wood, followed by a crocodile of officers. Saul, having finally got a signal, made some calls and arranged help. Soon he and Callum were in the force helicopter looking down on the widening search under them. Drift had come to a halt at an old mine entrance that was blocked and Saul asked Jim to take her home and look after her. They were circling around when Saul asked the observer, "What are those ruins there? They look like old buildings."

"The old lead mines, sir, this was the main entrance to them, closed off now so far as I know. Do you want to land there? The only access is a large tunnel but it is blocked off a couple of hundred metres further in."

"Sir, we train up here sometimes. I am pretty sure there are ways in, not known to many, mind."

"Thanks, Callum, yes, please put down there and let's see what we can find. Can we find a map?"

One was quickly produced and the observer pinpointed the location. As they landed, Saul said, "This is very close to the Birtwhistle farm. Sullivan will know this area. Get the dog units up to search."

On the ground, the search was underway. As the light began to fade one officer picked up some tyre tracks, and they followed them into an old but short tunnel where they found an old green Land Rover. By this time all useful light had gone, and Saul had to make a decision. He called off the ground and air search, and thought what to do. If he left any officers on the moor they were vulnerable to attack. If he withdrew until dawn, the chances were that Zoe and Diana might be dead. It was one of the hardest decisions he had had to make. He took Callum aside.

"You don't know anyone involved personally and can make a rational assessment of the situation. What would you do?"

"What you have done, sir. I would call out the cave rescue and get a map of the old mine workings. We will need caving gear to explore inside, but I do know the old workings stretched for miles, and are in very poor condition. They are also on several levels and go very deep. They are very, very dangerous and to rush in would put more lives in danger than are at the moment."

"Thank you. I agree. Call everyone in. I would like to have a base here, well-guarded, of course. Stand everyone else down and get them back for first light. We need to have some checkpoints on junctions on all approach roads, and I want someone to guard the Birtwhistle and Moorside Farm in case either Diana, Zoe or Sullivan turn up there. I want medical staff close by. We know one of them is injured. Some of these officers have been on duty for hours and will work better having had a rest. Senior officers and supervisors, we will have a debrief in ten minutes."

Saul stood thinking through his next step when his mobile rang. It was Sandra, ringing about the step daughter. Grateful of even the briefest distraction, he listened carefully to what she told him and then went to the coach that was used for transport of search teams, where they were to hold the debrief. Celia, Geoff and his other sergeant, Paul, were waiting with Callum and several other senior officers and supervisors. They knew the dilemma he was in and some of them privately thought they were glad it was his decision to make, and not theirs. One or two even thought that was why he got paid more than them.

"You all know what the situation is. May I have your honest comments please. Celia, record this, we may have to justify ourselves later. This is how I see it. We cannot find anything or anybody in the dark and the mine is too dangerous to enter until we are in the hands of experts. To leave people out in the open and exposed will put them in danger. We cannot help the two women who are missing without risking more lives. I am pretty sure now that our murderer is this Eddie Sullivan. Yes, Geoff."

"I do think we should keep observations and somewhere obvious for anyone in trouble to run to for help. From what we know of this Eddie is he is quite beyond reason, and out to hurt as many as possible. I will go into the mine if you want, at least to see if there are any tracks or signs."

Celia said, "Has it occurred to you that it might be Sullivan who is in danger, not the two women? Green has gone off on her own accord, she didn't want us around did she? I think she has done a runner. Probably with this Zoe girl and they might just have lured him into a trap, we know they both hate him. All we are working on is what SHE has told us in a hastily written account carefully hidden to slow us down. We don't even know it was her blood. You have to admit she is quite clever enough to have set such a trap."

There was a gasp from several of the people present. Saul frowned and said, "Yes, it had occurred to me, but there are things I know that you don't, and believe me if anyone is killed or injured when I could have prevented it I will never forgive myself if I made the wrong decision. Inspector Biddiscome, is there any way we can use some sort of heat-seeking gear to identify anyone moving round on the moor in the dark?"

"Not unless you want us chasing sheep all night, no, sir, there are thousands of them on the moor and the lambs as well. We could ask the chopper to go up with a heat-seeking camera from time to time that is about the best I can suggest. For that I believe we need the Chief's authority."

"Yes thank you, I hear what you all say. No. Geoff, you are not to go wandering into the mine. I will ring the chief now.

Stand the troops down, get them hot drinks and meals if they want them and I will ask for a skeleton staff to remain close and to act if anything transpires. We need them back at first light. I can't get a signal here so I am going up the hill a bit. My battery is low, can someone get me another phone or a new battery?"

Saul moved up the hill on a defined path and onto a ridge. He tripped on a heather root and the phone flew from his hand. He began to feel around when it rang, and he quickly answered it.

"Catchpole. Yes, Sandra, are you with her? Take her to the police station now, and her mother. When he rings by all means give him this number, but say I may be out of range. I'll be back at Hebden Police House in half an hour. Does he know you are with her? Good, don't mention it. How did he get your number, oh, I see? DON'T go back there. I'll make the arrangements."

Saul almost ran back down the hill.

"Leave the minimum cover here, everyone else, back to the police house. Someone, get this phone charged up somehow. I am waiting on a call. On this number, a very important one."

Chapter Six

Sandra was very shaken up. She turned to the girl with her and said, "Look, I want you to come with me now, it's very important. I'm ringing your mother to meet us. Eddie is coming after both of you so don't argue. I can keep you safe, but you must do as I say, now."

Karen Grady needed no persuasion, she went pale and began to shake. Quickly they got into Sandra's car and drove to the Police station, where two detectives were waiting for them. Before long Mrs Grady joined them having been fetched by other officers. Once they were safe, Sandra went to an office where she spoke to a Detective Inspector who was waiting for her.

"I have the bones of it from the guv'nor but I need you to tell me exactly what you told him."

"Yes, sir. I met Karen Grady at five this evening, just down the road from her house. I took her to the doctor's surgery, where she had a pregnancy test. It was positive. She was very frightened and upset. She told me she had been raped by Sullivan, and he had threatened to harm her and her family if she told anyone and to say it was consensual. I pleaded with her to tell her mother. In the end she agreed and I took her straight to the rape suite and WPC Drey dealt with it. We spent some time there. The mother then said she needed to do some shopping and would meet us back at their home. Karen had forgotten her mobile phone and wanted to ring a friend. I loaned her mine. We had a cup of coffee and were just leaving when I got a call on my phone. I pulled over and answered it, and as it was number withheld I put it straight onto record. It was a man with an Irish accent. He asked if I was a police officer. I said, yes, I was. He asked who was in charge of the murder case, and I said I didn't know, that I hadn't been told. He said, "Liar, I want to speak to the head pig, and tell him something. If I have to break in somewhere else to get his number I'll probably hurt someone, just to show I mean business. How do you think I got your number, bitch? Don't play games with me, little girl. You're the pretty one, with blonde hair and those lovely green eyes. I like green eyes. Sandra, ain't it? Who is in charge?"

I said, 'Chief Superintendent Catchpole. Can I get him to call you?

He said, 'I'm not stupid! No, I'll call you again very soon. Get his number, his personal number, and be ready to give it to me when I call. If you do that, little girl, then I won't hurt her, not 'till tomorrow anyway. You can tell him he will never find her.' I rang Mr Catchpole straightaway."

"So where did he get your number from?"

"There is only one place he could have got it, off Karen's phone, and that was at the Grady house. She put it there yesterday and I asked her where she had left it. She had the phone all day yesterday and until she came out today. She left it in her room when she came down to meet me. It was charging. She had logged me in her phone as Sandra, police, on her menu."

"How do you think he knows what you look like?"

"I wish I knew. I find it rather alarming."

"So do I. Do you live alone?"

"Yes I have a flat just down from the nick, above the newsagents."

"Well, for the moment, you are also under protective custody. If you need anything from home, we will get it for you. Until he rings back, sit quietly and have cup of coffee. I will stay with you. I am and you are under strict orders from the Chief Super. His exact words were, 'I cannot afford to lose or have one of my best officers threatened in any way. I need her. I have hopes she will become a permanent member of my squad. You look after her or I will have your guts for garters!' He meant it too. I know him quite well."

They sat and waited. Sandra began to write her statement about the matter and made her pocket book up, and the inspector checked it and signed and timed and dated it. After twenty-three minutes the phone rang. The inspector nodded and she answered.

"Have you got his number?"

"Yes he is expecting your call. It is 07771 676567."

"Aren't you a good little piggy? If you are lying, I'll get you or one of your porky friends. What is his first name?"

"Saul. I warn you, he is no fool."

"Sounds like a fucking Jew, is he?"

"I have no idea. Please don't hurt anyone."

"Shut up, bitch."

The line went dead. Sandra put the phone down and found she was sweating. The DI said, "Well done, lass, now that is your part over. Finish this statement and then go and relax in the rest room. Do not leave the station and don't go near the windows. We will move you to a safer place later."

"But, sir, I need to do something!"

"Then make another brew if you want."

Karen was talking to an older woman detective who took on the matters concerning the allegation of rape and despite the mother getting most agitated, calmed them both down and took them to a place of safety where they were certain of hiding from Eddie.

Jim took Drift back to the farm house and fed her and reassured her. He was reluctant to leave her out in the kennels so took her into the farm house with him and settled her in the kitchen. He cooked a meal and then an officer came, explained he was there to protect Jim and they settled down and watched the football together. Unfortunately, they each supported the opposite team, so they were well animated by the match. Jim went out brew a pot of coffee at half-time and unthinkingly left the kitchen door into the lounge open. Later, after the match had finished he noticed Drift happily asleep on the old leather arm chair by the radiator. He didn't have the heart to move her.

*

Zoe began trembling when she heard a slight noise coming from the passage. She wondered if he had come back to kill her. The candle had gone out long before and she had even managed to sleep for a while. She saw a flash of light down the passage and cowered back against the wall. Someone was creeping softly towards her and she wondered if this was just a trick to frighten her more. She waited, but there was no more light. She couldn't help it, she whimpered.

"Zoe, is that you? It's Diana. Are you alone?"

"Yes, please help me, be careful he may come back at any time."

"I know. Are you hurt?"

"A bit, where are you?"

"Close. I only have a small torch. I need to save the light."

"There are candles here but I can't reach them. Thank God you are here."

A small light came on, and Diana, quickly found the candles and lit one. She pocketed several others and then looked around. She grabbed Zoe's clothes from the pile and pushed them through the cage so Zoe could reach them.

"Put them on, as quick as you can. Are you warm enough?"

Zoe began to cry.

"Just about. He did leave me this sleeping bag."

"Big of him. Do you know where he keeps the key to this cage thing?

"He took it with him. I'm chained to the wall. He is going to kill me, I know he is."

"Not if I can help it! He has gone off somewhere in a car. Hang on, I'll see what I can find."

She looked around and soon gave a grunt of satisfaction, and came back with a metal crowbar, put it in the padlock on the door and with an effort broke the padlock, and came into the cage and put her hand on Zoe's shoulder and gave her a hug.

"Now, let's see how to get you out, child, stand back and pull when I say."

It took a little time but eventually she levered out the hasp in the wooden upright and Zoe could move. Zoe finished dressing as fast as she could. She was crying with relief.

"Thank you, I am so frightened. All he left me was a sleeping bag, one blanket and some water, is there another jumper over there? I am so cold."

"Yes, here, bring the bag, a blanket, there is one there, and any food. Wrap up what you can and leave the rest. I'll try to make it look like you are still here. We are not out of the woods yet and no one else knows exactly where we are. We can't go out that way, it's the way he uses and I don't want to meet him coming in. There is another way, I am sure, we just have to find it."

Together they quickly packed up what they needed in an old rucksack they found in the pile of clothes. Diana made a bundle in the blankets and Zoe collected what food she could find from a stash in a box she found. Diana said, "Is there a spare padlock in that lot?"

"Yes, two."

"Give them here, I will re-secure the door and keep the key. It will buy us a bit more time. Oh, well done you have found two torches. Any batteries? Oh there seem to be loads. You take one of the torches, and give me the second. Put new batteries in yours, and I will put my failing ones in his torch and use the new batteries in mine. Any spare batteries I will keep in my pocket, apart from one spare set I want you to keep in your pocket. Now come on, let's get out of here. Walk in my footsteps, literally I mean, so he thinks there is only one of us. Good God, child, have you nothing on your feet? Do you know where your shoes are?"

"I can't find them at all."

"OK, then this is what we do. I want you to walk a little distance until we are safe then we stop and sort it out. Walk carefully."

Zoe followed closely behind Diana as she walked carefully down the passage. As soon as they were some distance away from the cage, Diana found a side passage and slipped into it and pulled Zoe in, and motioned her to sit down out of sight round a corner. Diana took off her own boots and socks and handed them to Zoe.

"Put these on, and get warm. I can't have you dying of hypothermia."

She carefully went back into the main passage and walked some way to another junction turned right into another passage and went on until she came to a gaping hole in the floor, and then walked backwards in her own footsteps, until she once again joined Zoe, said, "I can't take your boots. What about you?"

"In a little while I will ask you for the socks back, but not yet. I think our feet are about the same size. You starting to warm up yet?"

"Yes and you have no idea how wonderful it feels. How can I thank you?"

"Actually I do know. By doing what I came here for, to get you to safety and get Eddie in prison. Before we go further I need to explain a couple of things. We must be very quiet or I won't hear anyone coming in time. Speak very softly, preferably whisper and then only if you must. Please, do as I ask, or we might just come very unstuck. Be brave, you have been so far, but right now tears are not going to help. I need you to trust me and do exactly what I say. I won't have the time to explain and might not be able to make any sound either. Can you do that?"

Zoe nodded frantically. Diana beckoned her to follow and carried on down the side passage, and they came to a junction. Diana carried on until they reached four more of these cross junctions and then turned right and soon they were back in the main passage again. Carefully walking on some boulders at the side of the passage they left no foot prints and after what seemed an age Diana sat down on a rock and listened for some minutes before whispering, "Can I have the socks back now? Keep the boots. Can you find me some food, something sweet? I am diabetic and I do need it. You have some too, but leave a little for later."

She pulled a tin out of her pocket and having eaten some biscuits handed to her by Zoe she injected herself and returned the tin to her pocket.

"Will you take the rucksack for a bit please? Let's move on. Keep the sides of the tunnel but don't touch any of the wooden uprights. They are not safe."

After a long and tedious length of passage it bent to the left and they saw the glint in the floor of metal and Zoe realized they were old rail tracks. A little further on there was a hollow in the wall and Diana went and sat down. She whispered, "Can you carry on, or do you need to rest? If we must stop, we will find somewhere and have a kip. Do you need to? Here give me the rucksack."

Zoe whispered, "No, I can carry on, are you OK?"

"Yes I am a tough old bird. Do you think the air is a bit fresher here?"

"I think I can smell grass and sheep."

"The sheep smell might be me, but the air is fresh and coming from that way. Let's move on."

They got up and carried on for some way until they were met by a huge boulder choke, and there appeared to be no way on. Zoe gasped and was about to cry. Diana grabbed her arm and whispered, "No, don't panic. I can't have you falling apart now. We are very close to the outside. He might be just out there. Please sit here, switch your torch off for a moment."

The darkness seemed to engulf them but as they looked around Zoe became aware of a very faint light above them a little back from the boulder fall. Diana saw it too and looked up. Then she moved away, and was gone a little while. Zoe began to tremble, but then heard a sort of dragging noise, and saw Diana's light down a side passage that she had not noticed before.

"Zoe, give me a hand please, and bring all the stuff."

Zoe gathered their things and switched her torch on and hurried down to where Diana was. Above them was a shaft and she could smell the heavenly scent of earth and grass. There was a faint light coming from a passage about ten metres up the shaft. It wasn't daylight and she was confused.

Diana whispered, "It is still night out there. Help me put this old ladder up. Then I want you to hold it while I test it out. If it is rotten I will have to find something else. Now keep as quiet as you can. Once I am up, I will throw you a rope. Tie it round the bag, and then yourself and I will help you up. Don't worry I won't let you fall. Once we are up we must switch off the lights. Here goes."

In the gloom it seemed that Diana almost levitated up the ancient and cracking ladder. At one point there was a crack and she slipped but somehow hung on. After what seemed an eternity, she heard Diana call.

"Here comes the rope. Tie it on the bag and you. Try not to touch the sides of the shaft they are very loose. Stand back."

With a sort of whizzing sound, the rope landed with a thud and Zoe rushed over, tied the bag to the end of the rope and then tied it round her waist. She was very grateful that a couple of months before she had gone with some students to a rock climbing centre. She remembered that Diana had been there that day and had climbed very well and even helped the others. She remembered and called out softly, "Take in."

When the rope became taut, she called, "That's me."

Diana called, "Climb when ready."

Zoe called back, "Climbing."

She was not a good climber and several times slipped and grabbed frantically at anything. At one point the rock she had tried to hold had dropped down and landed with a heart-stopping crash below her. She was held tight by the rope and finally got to the top of the climb and Diana pulled her up and onto safety in a small low tunnel.

"Light off"

Diana pulled the ladder up and put it on the ground and came and sat next to Zoe.

She whispered, "Well done. You remembered. That is stage one. Now we must be extra careful, because if we move we can be seen. If he is out there he will notice things like movement especially of sheep and animals. Don't stand above the sky line. Wait here. I am going for a recce. Untie the bag, coil the rope and keep warm. Back soon."

Diana crawled out into the fresh air and without a sound seemed to disappear into the night. Zoe hugged herself and tried to stop shivering. She was cold but was also trying to overcome the terror of what had happened, and the relief that at last something had changed. Suddenly Diana was back beside her.

"Come on, slowly and very quietly. Bring the bag. Leave the rope please."

They wriggled out into the fresh air and Zoe thought the sight of stars above them was the most wonderful sight she had ever seen. On all fours they crawled away from the low entrance and up a slight track that looked and smelled as if it was made by sheep, until they reached a small rock outcrop with a small stream cascading down it.

Zoe whispered, "What do we do now?"

"Move away from here as fast as we can. I need to get a phone signal and put you somewhere safe, very safe. Bring the bag, make as little noise as you can. Don't whatever you do shine a light. It could be seen for miles."

*

Saul sat waiting for the call. If he was nervous, he didn't show it. He had been told what Sandra had said to Eddie and wondered exactly who Eddie was referring to as 'she'. If he intimated he didn't know, then he might alert Eddie to Diana's presence somewhere nearby. He was worried that both the women were in grave danger, and there was little he could do until dawn to help them. The phone rang, and as he had already switched it to record, he let it ring four times before he answered.

"Catchpole."

"You must be Saul then. The head pig, the yid. I've got her and if you don't back off I'll kill her."

"Kill who?"

"You know. Don't play games with me. Silly bitch thought she could throw me over. No one makes a fool of me. Stop looking for me or I will take out one of yours as well. I want to talk to Karen, where is she?"

"Safe. Look, Eddie, you won't get away. Why not give yourself up? I can't do a deal with you and I will not put anyone else at risk. I'll meet you, if you want, you won't be harmed if you give yourself up. What started all this anyway?"

"And walk into your trap? No. Tell Karen I want to talk to her. I want to know if it's mine. If it is I might let her live. She won't answer the phone, and isn't at her home. If you get her to talk to me I will tell you where that bitch of an ex-pig is, or at least where her body is. I know I shot her. I found the blood but she crawled away to die."

"We have already found Diana Green's body. That's four you have killed. Why did you kill Grady?"

"He betrayed me. Just because I was dating his silly daughter. I was all right to work for him on his scam, but not good enough to be with his precious little step daughter. He didn't even know who I was until I told him. Don't try to trick me."

"Why did you kill Billy and Mc Gill?"

"They upset me. No one upsets me and gets away with it."

"What makes you so special?"

"I am clever. More than you know, I always have been. Don't try to trace this call, it won't work. I will ring you again, if only to tell you how I killed Zoe. Makes you feel helpless does it? Good. Her death will be on your conscience. You didn't think I actually wanted to know about sheep, did you? I am far more important than that. I will be a hero."

The call ended. Saul put the phone down and handed it to the technical officer next to him, who transferred the recording and handed it back to him.

"Did we get a trace?"

"Only that it is within fifteen miles from here. The number was blocked. At least he admitted it."

"Yes but it doesn't help much. He doesn't know Diana is still alive. He won't be looking for her, providing he believed me, that is. Now we have to wait. Any chance of a coffee? Is my phone fully charged?"

"Yes, sir, and here is a spare charged battery."

As the phone was handed back to Saul, it rang. Saul looked at it and said, "I think that is Diana's number. I hope it isn't him again, that would mean he has her. Catchpole."

"It's Diana Green. I am safe, so is Zoe. I got her out of the old lead mines."

"Where are you?"

"That is the problem, I am not sure. We are hiding up on the moor. It won't be long till it is light. Then I might be able to tell you. I will ring you back, my battery is getting low. I can't talk long. Is my dog all right?"

"Yes, we found her in the cave."

"I can hear a vehicle. I must go. I'll ring you back."

Saul gave a sigh of relief, he made several calls, and dozed in his chair for a while, as everyone else set up his plan.

Chapter Seven

Zoe was shivering, and hungry. They had finished the food, and it was just getting light. Diana was sitting immobile like a small hunched-up statue, watching. They had talked for a while and then she had gone off, and returned, putting her finger to her mouth to insist on total silence. Zoe could hear the noise of an engine in the distance. She looked at Diana, and gasped. She saw the bloody mess of cloths and rags wrapped round Diana's arm, for the first time.

"Oh God, Di, you're hurt. Let me look at it for you."

"I'll live, best not to start it bleeding again. Thanks but not now. Listen, that engine is coming closer. I heard it just now, in the distance when I was up near the ridge. Don't show yourself."

Together they peered over the bank and saw a four-wheel drive vehicle, without any lights bouncing up a track beneath them. It stopped in an old quarry and they saw Eddie get out, and walk off to their left, behind a buttress of rock. He had a rifle in his hand. He was far too close for comfort and Zoe hissed, "I want to go, now, please before he finds us!"

"If we move now he'll see us or the sheep moving away from us. That must be another entrance to the mine down there.

He is about to miss you, but it will take him a while to work out what has happened. I need to hide you, in case he knows the way out we used. If he does come looking, I'll draw him away, but you must promise me that whatever happens, you will not show yourself. Now, wriggle down in the sleeping bag, under that rock there under the overhang, in that crack. I'll cover you with moss and grass. Watch and listen. If he does spot me, you must stay put."

"You could be killed. Why would you do that for me?"

"I'll tell you later. If anything does happen to me find a good home for my dog, and for his."

"I can't let you do this. I thought it was me he was after."

"Will you shut up? If push comes to shove I wouldn't hesitate to kill him, but you would. You must lie totally still and silent or you will put us both in danger. There, even I can't see you. I won't be far and don't come out unless I tell you to or a uniformed policeman does. Trust me."

She had gone. Zoe couldn't even hear her as she slithered away. It was quite warm in her snug crack and she rested her head so she could just see through the grass to the bank opposite her. She must have dozed off because the light was much stronger when she was woken by an angry shout from quite nearby. She froze with fear and knew Eddie was close by.

"You bitch, think you can get away from me do you? Come out now from where you are hiding or I'll make you pay for it. I'll be nice to you if you give up. If I find you, you will wish you were dead."

She began to tremble when he walked into the ditch beside her. He still had the gun, she could see the barrel, and knew it was a rifle. He paused and turned smartly and lay down on the bank in front of her, with his back to her and raised the gun. She was within a couple of metres of him, and she could see him through the thick moss and grasses hiding her. He took aim, fired twice, swore and then jumped up over the ditch and ran off down the hill. After a few minutes, she heard a helicopter overhead, and it was hovering nearby. There were men shouting. She waited. Then more voices and car engines and what sounded like a quad bike. She considered revealing herself but remembered what Di had said. She waited.

*

Saul had been much relieved when Diana had rung again, and it was getting light. He was already at the bottom of the moor, where the search teams were assembling. He was looking at the wide expanse of the moor with a pair of binoculars when he saw movement. It was a long way away and looked like someone crawling along a ridge. He pointed in the direction and at the same time heard two distinct shots, and then saw another figure further up the moor. The helicopter moved in, and hovered over the area. A line of officers and dogs moved over towards that part of the moor. Saul looked round and Callum was driving the police Land Rover rapidly towards him, and stopped to let Saul get in and drove up the barely discernible track, with a skill and at a speed that Saul would never have attempted. They arrived where Saul had seen the first movement, at about the same time as several officers and their dogs. One dog handler said, "I'm sure it was about here, sir, I saw someone fall. Do you want the dog to find them?"

"You don't need to, it's all right that was me. Mr Catchpole, have you anything to eat please, chocolate or something. It's OK she is safe, I will take you to her. She won't come out of hiding unless I call her."

Diana stood up not five metres from him out of a clump of rushes. Saul called, "Has anyone anything sweet please, urgently."

Someone produced a Mars bar and handed it to him and he unwrapped it for her and she took a bite out of it. She said, "Come, I'll show you. Is this officer armed because he is still around."

"Yes, Diana, and so am I. Come with me, Callum, and you two. Someone bring the Land Rover."

He almost had to sprint up the hill after her and then they were in a hollow. He looked round but could see nothing except some large boot footprints in a patch of mud and some metal glistening on the edge of the bank.

"It's all right, Zoe, you can come out now, the police are here and you are safe. Before you go could I have my wellies back please?"

Several officers helped Zoe as she scrambled out of her hiding place, and they ushered her to the waiting Land Rover which had just made it up the track nearby and had turned round to go back down. They sat her in the back and wrapped a blanket round her.

Diana said, "Please get her to safety as soon as you can."

Saul nodded to them and they drove off down the track. He turned round just in time to see Diana sit down rather abruptly on the bank. He looked at her and said, "I want an explanation from you, officer. You are, still, aren't you? Hang on, I think you are hurt. Is it bad?"

"Not too good, actually. He just got me again in the shoulder. He has gone back into the mine, call the dogs off or they will get hurt. He knows that mine very well. You will lose a dog if they run free round here, there are shafts everywhere."

"You haven't given me an answer. I'll get the medics. Lie down, woman, you are as white as a sheet. Don't you dare faint on me!"

As she lost consciousness, he grabbed her, called for help, and found the wound on her shoulder from which blood was flowing. He took his handkerchief from his pocket, thanking fate that it was clean, and pressed it against the bullet wound in her right shoulder. Other officers rushed to help him and soon the helicopter had landed nearby and the medics took over. Celia had arrived in another Land Rover and rushed up to him. Saul stood back, barked out a few orders at the increasing number of officers arriving telling them to return to the rendezvous point. He moved towards the waiting helicopter as the medics carried Diana on a stretcher, having put a drip line in.

"Celia, take over. He's back in the mine. It stretches for miles and there are numerous ways in and out. Take advice from Callum here and make sure anyone left here has bullet proof clothes on. Otherwise stand most of the troops down. I need to go with her."

"Why, I can get a WPC to be at the hospital. Surely you should stay in charge here, and send a junior officer, after all she is only a suspect."

"I can't tell you why but I need to be with her."

He climbed into the helicopter and soon it was taking off. As it flew away Callum said, "You *are* brave Ma'am. May I point out the two cartridge cases here on the bank? I know why he has to go with her, but it is for him to tell you, when he sees fit. I wouldn't dream of telling someone of his rank and reputation what to do."

*

Diana began to come round as they approached the helipad at the hospital. She looked at him, murmured,

"Not now, I'll tell you later."

And went back to sleep.

As Diana was being treated Saul made arrangements for her protection. He knew that in due course she would tell him, but until them he had to be vigilant, and protect her and everyone else involved. A doctor came out and told him that she was no longer in danger and asked if she had any next of kin who should be informed. He said he didn't know but to put him down as such. He waited outside the private room where she was, and would not move until a uniformed officer came to relieve him. Even then he was not gone long, merely cleaning himself up and arranging for a change of clothes to be brought to him and some paperwork.

It was about an hour after that, when he was sitting reading a report outside the room when he got a call on his phone. It was Eddie, and Saul instantly put it on record.

"Think you are very clever don't you, telling me she was dead. I hope she is now. If I can't have either of those I'll kill every policewoman I see. Yes, I will have to lie low for a while, but I'll be back, you Yiddish pig."

Saul had not been racially abused for some time and was quite gratified that he had rattled Eddie that much. He waited in the relatives' room and then dozed off. A nurse woke him a couple of hours later saying Diana had asked to see him and had said the other officer wouldn't do. He entered the room and saw Diana hooked up to various tubes. He looked down at her. The nurse tactfully left the room. He said, "Well, do I get an answer?"

"I need you to make a call for me. From my phone. It has to start with a text. Then you will get an explanation, but not necessarily from me. I can't do it, my fingers are not free or working too well just now. The phone will need charging first."

He sat on the seat by her bed and wrote down exactly what she told him, and then took her phone, found a charger, charged it up sufficiently and the tapped in the text, sent it and took it back to her.

"Wait, they will ring back. I must speak to them first, then they will give you some instructions."

Within five minutes the phone rang, and he held it to her face.

"Little lambs eat ivy. Frogs like ponds. Yes, but I'm hurt. I need you to talk to the man with me. He's twigged, and now wants an explanation. He's not happy at all with me, or you."

She indicated for him to continue the call and he identified himself, answered some questions, and then said, "Understood. No I won't argue. Too right I am furious about it. When and where? Yes, she is. Why there? All right I'll talk to her and explain. I don't see why I should but she is hurt so I won't brow beat her. I'll get her moved. I have one of those. I'm sticking to her like glue."

When the call had finished he said, "We are moving you and I am coming with you. Once there you are going to explain. Are you really diabetic?"

"Yes, I am. Is Zoe all right?"

"Yes, thanks to you. Will you tell me what I need to know? They say you will."

"At this moment no one, not even your chief needs to know. They will be told, by someone else."

Saul looked at her in amazement. She had unnerved him before, but now she scared him.

"I understand, you have my promise, I think if I let you out of my sight I will never find you again. Is that right?"

"Probably, but no I need your help. You need mine. Get some rest, and so will I."

He found it really annoying when she promptly went to sleep on him. He found some benches outside the room and followed her example.

Chapter Eight

Celia relished the challenge of coordinating the search for Sullivan. It was a massive operation, and her particular skill was with logistics. What she didn't understand was why Saul had dumped the whole thing in her lap without explanation. She had learned a great deal from him over the previous two years and she thought she was a better officer for it. Another thing she was at a loss over was that although the rest of the squad were correct, polite and obedient and efficient they suddenly seemed not to want to chat to her and were apparently avoiding her. She organized the search of the mine, having found an ancient map, which helped a lot, and the Cave Rescue, which had been suggested by Callum, were a great help. They found five more entrances, where Zoe had been kept, and where the two women had escaped, which was very close to one entrance which was two side passages from the big boulder choke. She was a bit annoyed that Callum had told her it might be good idea to get DNA samples from the items obviously used by Eddie. She should have thought of that. Callum made no secret that he did not care for her. The team had found a quad bike, reported stolen some months before, in the mine together with a motor cycle with the Vehicle

Identification numbers ground off. She had them sent off for examination by the stolen vehicle squad. The whole mine was checked but Sullivan was not in it. All but one entrance was blocked, and the remaining one was secured and fitted with a silent alarm.

Celia took a call from Saul, asking for an update and he promised to ring back that evening, but again he wouldn't tell her why he was occupied elsewhere. She was a little offended and felt he didn't trust her. She broached the matter with Geoff.

His answer shocked her.

"You see, ma'am, we would all of us follow the guv'nor into hell and back, even if he didn't want us to. Nor would we openly challenge his judgement the way you did. He obviously knew things you and we were not privy to. Your obvious hostility to Green was like a challenge to his judgement. You should have expressed your doubts to him privately. He would have listened, he always does. Green read you very accurately and you don't like it. If I didn't know better, I would say you were jealous of the esteem he obviously holds her in. You know you are the only member of the squad that has not been personally hand-picked by him? You were imposed on him, the second in command often is. Now you feel he doesn't trust you and you are hurt by it. If he didn't trust you he would not have left you in charge. There were plenty of other senior officers around he could have asked. He knows your strengths better than you think. He also knows the weaknesses of every one of us. Some of us even know his weaknesses too. We keep our knowledge to ourselves. Stop resenting Callum Doyle, too. You may not know but he is due to be promoted to Inspector.

Mr Catchpole saw in him something he needed. You won't like this, but you asked me so I am going to tell you straight. Grow up. You made a prize prat of yourself, from the moment you went out to a farm with high-heeled patent leather shoes, to obviously thinking you know better than the rest of us. The only person that can put this right is you, with the help of Saul. It will help if you apologize to him, but he wouldn't want you to do it in public. Until you can do that don't expect the rest of the squad to be your best mates. Point taken?"

*

Eddie was very angry that he had to lay low, it was inhibiting him severely. Not only had he lost Zoe but he wasn't sure he had killed Diana. It had shaken him when he saw her on the moor, as he thought she was already dead. Then the police had turned up a bit too quickly on the moor, and he had only just made it through and out of the mine in time before they had flooded the whole area with dogs and men. He had managed to grab his stores, weapons and money and was now hiding up. This was just one of the escapes he had planned if ever anything went wrong. He needed the cover of darkness to move again. Now he was taking refuge in an old water reservoir pump house by the river. He had hidden his motor cycle round the back out of sight. He was tired so he grabbed the cushions off a chair and got his head down.

*

Albert Gatsby had worked for the water board for years. He was a glorified handyman and caretaker for all the buildings in the area. He had a radio in his van and was well aware of the man hunt in progress. He had already been stopped three times and his van searched and he had been closely questioned. He had a photograph of Sullivan on his dash board. He thought he was well out of the search area and his last call was the quarterly check on the old pump house. It wasn't used now but needed to be kept safe. He pulled down the lane just after five, and got his tools out and hunted for the key on his keyring. He walked towards the building and paused. The small window was steamed up, which he had never seen before. He was about to investigate when he paused. The door lock had been forced. Silently he crept away and made it back to his van which was just out of sight of the pump house. He radioed what he had found to his control room. The police were saying this man was dangerous and he was taking no chances!

He waited, watching the lane. He was impressed when suddenly there was a police motorcyclist standing by his driver's door. He wound the window down, and was told to drive to the next cross road where he would be met by another officer. He did exactly as he had been asked to and when he got to the crossroad there was a great deal of police activity. Even a helicopter. He drew a basic plan of the pump house for a kind inspector and handed over the keys to the van and the pump house key. He was driven to the local police house in the next village and was well looked after by the lady of the house who made a very acceptable cup of tea and coffee cake.

It was the helicopter that woke Eddie. He peered out of the small window and smiled to himself. They must be spending a fortune on trying to catch him! He took a hefty swig from the bottle of Southern Comfort he had, and ate some sandwiches. Then he needed to pee, so did so all over the old fireplace. He sat down and planned his next move, when he was going to get over to the next dale and then to a deserted farm house high up on the moor. No one went up there, not after dark.

He heard the van approaching and glanced at it as it blocked the lane. It was a water board van, and he cursed his luck. He thought quickly and decided the van would suit his purpose better. He would kill the driver, which would give him time to get away. The driver seemed intent on doing paper work in the cab, so he got his gear together, and slowly opened the door and crept out. If he stuck to the bushes he could creep up and shoot the man before he was noticed. The cover was very thick, and he was so self-confident, he knew it would be easy. With his hand gun in his jacket pocket he moved silently out from the doorway and into the thicket of elders and hawthorn, and crouched down under an old and substantial tree to get ready to move. The weight that hit him of two very large and determined policemen, from the tree above, knocked the wind out of him and before he could move they had handcuffed him. They were bigger and quicker than him, and had dragged him out and had searched him and found the gun. They next went for the knife he kept in his boot, that they obviously knew was there. Eddie knew who had told them about that! Lights came on from all over the place and there were coppers everywhere, including one from the van, who approached him and said,

"Edward George Joseph Sullivan, you are under arrest for the murder of Michael John Grady."

An officer began to caution him, and Eddie spat vigorously at him, struggled violently kicking one officer on the shin, the officer hardly flinched, as he was wearing body armour. Three policemen had guns aimed at him, and from their expressions he knew they would use them. He relaxed and said, "You've got the wrong man. I don't know who you think I am, but my name is Charles Avington. I saw the door ajar and went in to see what the matter was, you are searching for someone I know, I thought I would check it out and then call you. I found the gun in there. I'll be honest, I was hoping to do a bit of poaching which is why I had the knife. I don't think they have been long gone, you might catch him if you hurry."

He never thought it would fool them but it was worth a try. A woman in civilian clothes walked up from the road and said, "That's him. Take him to the nick and search him very thoroughly, a strip search."

"Yes, ma'am."

"Don't take your eyes off him for a second. Cuff his ankles. He has nothing to lose by killing the lot of us."

He was put into a prison van and in the opposite cage was an officer with a gun trained on him. As the van drew away and a forensic team went into the pump house, Celia said, "That worked well! I will ring the guv'nor and tell him. I will leave you to mop up, Terry, you take over please. De-brief at the station in a couple of hours. I have work to do."

After she had gone someone was heard to mutter, "I notice she forgot to ask if we were all right and if anyone was hurt. He would have. Stuck-up bitch."

Albert got his van back within the hour and the thanks of the police. He felt quite proud of himself, until he got home late and his wife had a go at him. He had to drag her in front of the television when the news was on, to convince her he had been doing his public duty. Only then did she relent, and let him go down the pub where he didn't have to buy a pint all night. Once again his wife moaned at him when he got home and he slept on the sofa.

Chapter Nine

Saul woke with a start when a nurse gently shook him. He had slept most of the day and his initial reaction was one of panic that Diana had gone. The nurse, gently removing the blanket she had covered him with some hours before, reassured him.

"She wants to talk to you, she has rested and is much better. I tried to wake you earlier but all I could do was cover you up and put a pillow under your head. You must have been exhausted, and your colleagues said to leave you. They have kept guard for you."

Diana was sitting up and trying to struggle into clothes. The nurse said, "Oh, no you don't. You have some nasty injuries. The doctor said three days, remember?"

"Yes I heard what he said, but I have to go. I'll sign anything you want."

Saul looked at her.

"If they say three days then that is how long it will be. What is the rush? You are quite safe here, I promise."

"I don't doubt it but that is not why I have to go. We can't talk here. I have unfinished business to sort out. You too. Just take me away, please. If you are worried, I'll come back if I get any worse. I'm actually quite tough you know."

"I'd worked that out. Where do you want to go?"

"Somewhere safe, a hotel or even a cell block if it makes you happier. I am not going to run away from you, I promise. I need you and you need me. I will explain but not here."

"Nurse, is she likely to die on me if she leaves?"

"I doubt it, she just needs rest and to relax. The bullets have been removed and your fellows have them, she has antibiotics, and an anti-inflammatory. She needs somewhere safe and to relax, which she hasn't done for a moment here. She will be in a bit of pain, I will get some pain killers from the doctor, and some fresh insulin, if she really must go."

"Stop talking about me as if I wasn't here. Yes, it is sore but believe me I have had worse. Pain killers are gratefully accepted. I do want to leave please."

Saul gave in. He said, "Give me ten minutes will you? I need to get transport. Nurse, don't let her go until I come back."

He went out of the room and rang his wife.

"Darling, I'm sorry I have been tied up. I need a big favour I need to bring us a house guest, a woman also called Diana. She is sort of a fellow officer and she needs a safe haven. Thanks, I knew you would understand, and I love you. Can you get the guest room ready?"

His next step was to ring for a taxi and then he went in and picked up Diana's bag and said, "We had better get you signed out and then I am taking you to a safe place. Come on, do you need a wheelchair? All right! There is no need to glower at me like that, I only asked!"

The discharge took about thirty minutes but finally they were in the back of a taxi. Saul asked, "Why do I get the impression you have done this before? I'll tell you now that I saw some of the scars you have, when I was trying to stop the bleeding. You have been in the wars haven't you?"

"You could say that, it is not the first time I have been shot, no. I have no idea where we are going."

"Good! Now I want to take a few precautions so we will swap taxis in a bit and then again before we arrive."

"I agree. It would seem you have read the handbook. Thanks for saving my life by the way. You were that cross with me several times I didn't really deserve it."

"True, but thank you for saving that child, Zoe. That was very brave. Why?"

"She is a nice kid and I could. That's why. You couldn't put any officer at that risk and it needed to be done quickly. I must say you cottoned on very fast. I knew you would but your woman officer didn't. I am sorry but I think she is a stuck-up rather shallow woman. Now where is my dog?"

"Quite safe, I assure you. My inspector doesn't like you much either, she is convinced that you are the murderer. Actually it was a skipper who cottoned on, he pointed out to me the blatantly obvious. He is ex-SAS. He said, when we had been in the cave that you must have been trained to do what you were doing. It was only then the penny dropped."

"Then you need to use that officer."

It took an hour before they pulled up in a rather secluded and very posh close, and Saul took her bag and let her into a large modern detached house, with a drive and lawned garden to the front with some shrubs in a bed, and he opened the front door, called out to someone that he was home, and then showed her into a large and well-furnished lounge. He asked her to sit down on the settee, while he drew the curtains of the front windows and opened a door towards the back of the house. Two large and boisterous golden Labradors rushed in and immediately sniffed at Diana, and then sat beside her, obviously guarding her. Saul looked at them and frowned.

"They have never done that before. Do you have this effect on all animals? They are guarding you!"

"I wish! No, dogs and horses and cats. I wish it worked with sheep. Where am I?"

"My house, ah, hallo, darling! This is my wife, who is also called Diana, but I call her Anna."

"And I am Di, to my friends."

He caught a sly glance from her as she shook hands with his wife, and he said, "You mean, just at the moment, all right I won't press it. I am arranging that my things are brought home for me. What do you need fetched?"

"Bless you, I do need some clean clothes and my spare insulin. Some night gear would be handy. They are all in my room at college or at the farm but there isn't much there. Ask Bryony, the warden, she will get what I need. I'd rather it was her."

Saul disappeared into another room.

"Until then, Di, I can lend you some things. You are about the size of my eldest daughter who is away at school. In fact you are a little smaller and there is plenty of stuff she has outgrown, if you are not offended. You look rather bloody, do you want a bath or shower? Look, come up to the room I have prepared for you, and I'll run you a shower or bath. If I can call you Di, then you call me Anna, it is what Saul calls me anyway."

"Thank you, I am sorry to impose. Does he often do this, bring home lame dogs?"

"Occasionally, but I don't mind. I am pleased to help, if you want my help."

"I could use some, yes, I am not supposed to get the bandages wet. I've no washing things with me. Have you a spare flannel?

"Plenty. Come on."

"I would offer to buy it, but I have no money at the moment. I ought to ask him to get some for me at a cash point. My card is at the farm."

"You don't buy it here! I'll ask him, you get undressed as far as you can, and I'll come back and help you. He is in the study now making phone calls. Are you in this force?"
"No, I used to be an officer in another force. We are in the same line of work, you might say."

"I'll get a laundry basket. These things are going in the wash now. It's all right, I have two rugby-playing sons so I am not shocked!"

They both laughed and half an hour later Di came downstairs in a pair of pyjamas with teddy bears on them, a Wonder Woman dressing gown, and a pair of Gromit slippers that were much too big for her, but fitted as her feet were covered in bandages. Saul had also changed into slacks and a rather comfy-looking shirt and jumper and had opened some wine, a bottle of red and one of white. There were slices of bread and a pasta salad ready on the dining room table. He said, "Say what you want, and is it red or white?"

"Red please. Thanks."

He filled a glass, and spooned out food onto a plate, and she sat at the table and started to eat. Saul's mobile went off, and he went and looked out of the windows as he listened for a while. He turned round, looked at her and smiled.

"Thank God for that! Well done, to everyone. No one got hurt? Good. Do you need me to come in? Good, she is safe, I know where but am not telling anyone. I am taking the rest of the evening off. I am at home if you want me. Is Zoe all right? Tell my B&B I'll come in and settle up in the next few days, oh you already have. Thanks for that, Terry. Good forward planning. Are you off home? Sure, don't knacker yourself."

"We have Eddie in custody, no doubt it is him, and everyone else is safe and unhurt."

He saw Di relax visibly. The taut demeanour he had always seen seemed to melt away. She nodded and turned her head away. She gave an almost shy smile and when she turned her head back to look at him, he saw tears in her eyes. Tears of relief. That scared him more than anything else she had done. They were about the same age, but suddenly he saw a very vulnerable isolated woman in front of him. His wife was ahead of him, and sat beside Di, put her arm around her and said, "It is all right, you are safe now. We will look after you. You've had a very rough time for a long time?"

Di nodded and gave a wry smile, and suddenly Saul saw the real woman sitting in front of him. He wondered what to do, but his wife seemed to have it under control, and passed Di some tissues and waved Saul away, out of the room. In that instant he knew he had done the right thing to bring her to his home.

About twenty minutes later they came into the lounge and Saul immediately refilled her glass.

"Better now?"

"Much, thanks. You are both very kind. Sorry I shouldn't have let go, but I have been trying not to be murdered for the last nine months. Then suddenly I am safe from my two most obvious assassins. It is a bit of a shock. Do you have a back garden?"

"Yes, why?"

"Could I go out there for a few moments?"

"If you want to be alone, you could use the study, your room, the dining room, the conservatory or we can go into the kitchen?"

She laughed.

"No, it's not that, I would like a smoke and won't do it inside. You look shocked that I smoke, Anna, you see I worked out some time ago that I am unlikely to make it to old age and smoking wouldn't have time to kill me. So I enjoy one occasionally, but not of course when the aroma might betray me, or in other people's houses. I wouldn't dream of lighting up here. My fags are in my pocket. Mr Catchpole, could I first ring the farm and speak to Jim, tell him I'm OK and check on my dog?"

Saul laughed and said, "Yes of course, I smoke a cigar or cheroot occasionally in the conservatory. But if it must be the garden go ahead. The patio has seats and a table and even an ashtray out there. Jim told me that Drift had taken up residence in his sitting room. He says she is house trained. You love that dog don't you?"

Diana nodded, and went out to the conservatory, with Anna. Then she ventured out to the patio and sat quietly for some time, enjoying her cigarette. Meanwhile, Saul made some more calls. When Di came back and sat in the conservatory, Saul joined them lit a cheroot and said, "Do you want to ring Jim?"

"He won't be in from the barn yet, I'll ring later, now I know she is safe."

Anna said, "I have to go out soon. I have an evening class to teach at the college. There is a casserole in the oven for later. Saul can deal with it. You need a proper meal, Di, it looks like you haven't had one in a while?"

"I hadn't really thought about it. I do eat, regularly, I have to, but a home-cooked meal – that is heaven!"

Di dozed off, while Saul checked on the oven and did other tasks and then went to his study. The dogs lay at Di's feet, which Saul found rather perplexing, they normally lay beside him if he was working in the study. It was about an hour later when Saul had checked on Di and the doorbell rang. The dogs barked and Di woke up and immediately tensed up. Saul could see her doing it. He went to the front door and minutes later in rushed Drift, found Di in the living room, and squinnying with pleasure, cuddled up to her. The other dogs, having had the usual smelling introduction joined her and together they made a large foot warming carpet around Di, who sat on the sofa and placed a hand on Drift's head. Once again Saul saw tears, and handed her a box of tissues.

"Thank you, from the bottom of my heart!"

Saul then brought in some other things from the hall, including a dog bed, blanket, bowls and food, and handed Di some carrier bags of clothes and a small suitcase.

"I'm just going to dish up supper, but I'll put the dog bed and food and bowls in your room. I'd better or my two will eat the food. I take it the blanket is hers? OK. Come through to the dining room when you are ready, do you want these clothes and case up there too?"

"Thanks, I'll just get a couple of things out of them first, there, that's all I need for now. I can take them."

"No, you can't. Let me. You are supposed to take things easy and if you don't I will cart you back to hospital. Just accept it. I am not going to give in on this."

"Bully. I capitulate."

"Well, I think that is a first! Behave, woman! Do as you are told for once in your life. Here, my stick. I had to use it last year when I broke my leg, hence the limp. I think it might help you."

They ate in companionable silence and after the meal, Di took out her insulin tin, opened it, and tested her blood, and duly injected herself in her calf. Saul stared at the open tin, and said, "I must remember to instruct my officers to be more observant and to know how to search properly in future. Someone, Celia, should have spotted that."

Diana shut the tin, smiled wickedly at him and said, "Yes I think you should, but you are the first one to notice it."

"I think I know what the pill is for, unfortunately, but the second syringe, that sealed one, oh of course, the antidote."

"Keep it to yourself please. Now can I wash up?"

"No, you can't. I have a perfectly adequate dishwasher. I'll just load it, make yourself comfortable in the lounge because we need to talk."

Once back in the lounge he refilled their glasses and sat down and said, "Right, Diana, if that is really your name, I think you have some serious explaining to do. Yes, let Drift sit on the sofa beside you, I doubt I could move her and my dogs go on there, sometimes."

"Yes, I know I do. I have the authority to tell you now, I didn't before. You are apparently of a sufficient security rank, now, to know. I can't tell you all of it by any means, but you have probably gathered there is something much, much bigger going on around the college. You see, my job isn't finished yet, I have to go back, and complete what I was sent to do. I also would like to get the qualification, because they keep saying I can retire soon and I will need it, when this is all over. I take it you know who you were talking to earlier? Yes, I thought so."

"I know what it means and the implications of it. I must admit what he told me shocked me, badly. It was him who told me to protect you at all costs and just how vital you are, and how stupidly brave you are and how tough. He said to take you to where other senior officers didn't have right of access. That did shake me. I can't know too much or I might give something away. You suspect someone in this force don't you? More than one I think. Am I suspected?"

"No. You were never a suspect you know. You are so detached from every day policing. Not part of the usual system of things. The murders were totally unexpected and a nuisance, but by their nature they have moved the goal posts. Eddie going psycho has made things very difficult."

"Did you always know he was the killer?"

"Not at first, no. When Nick told me Mike had been found, I thought it was probably Eddie. Even then I wasn't sure. What I didn't expect was that you would suspect me so quickly. When you first came up to see me, I already knew about Mike. I was expecting you, well a junior rank to be honest, at some time. I had put some things in place, like in the cave, just in case. I am so relieved Eddie is in custody. By the way make sure he doesn't have a pill, like the one you just tumbled. He might. You need to do a really detailed search and give him nothing of his own in custody. Eddie has been trying to kill me for months, not because he suspected me, but because he didn't like me. They made a bad mistake recruiting him he is far too unstable."

"Will he talk do you think?"

"I doubt it. I don't think he would dare. If he did I doubt he would last long. He knows that. Not about that, about the murders, he will probably boast about them. He has lost sight of what his role is. There are bigger fish to fry, believe me. Bigger, more powerful and much more dangerous. If he had known why I was really there, I would have been dead weeks ago. Someone would have got me, not necessarily him. He just hated me for being an ex-copper. It is wise to stick to as much of the truth as you can, you know. It was quite a good cover, because it made my attitude believable."

"Was Grady involved? Before you tell me, I think I need to tell someone that Eddie must be kept in solitary confinement, in case someone gets to him. Am I right?"

"Quite right."

When Saul returned, Diana said, "Oh yes, Grady was involved. It took me a while to work it out. One of my briefs was to make life difficult for them. I think I did that rather well!"

"I think so too. Do you think the bodies being put on the railway line is of any importance?"

"You just had to ask me that, didn't you? The one question I didn't want you to. I had to do some quick thinking about them."

"You were responsible for moving the bodies?"

"I might have been, not directly, but it was my idea. We didn't want you dealing with the murders. We wanted British Transport to do it. They would have taken longer, if they had ever got to the bottom of it. They don't have your reputation."

"I know enough to know you are not working alone. Is there anyone I should be, shall we say, very gentle with?"

"In other words who is my accomplice? I can't tell you that. I can tell you who not to suspect."

"It'll do, carry on. More wine?"

"You won't get me drunk, you know. I have the capacity of an elephant, through years of practice. This is a very good wine. OK, you know Nick the shepherd is such a nice man."

"Is he? He certainly put me in my place. Nick moved Grady I think. I doubt we could prove it. Or that he will admit it."

"Wonderful man! Janet, she has nothing to do with this and is a wonderful shepherd, a bit shy and very bright. We have become good and genuine friends. If you can, please leave her alone. She isn't one of us. You need not bother with Amy, Alex, David or Bryony. Nor are they. Just ordinary folk. The new principal, Hardaker, I don't think he is anything to do with anything, but I can't be sure. Zoe may know things that Eddie has told her, but she is an innocent victim and doesn't know what she knows. I think I do now. I had a long chat with her in the mine, and I am sure of it. She was just a plaything to Eddie, but I will tell you she is very brave. It took a lot for her to survive what she did, and then she had me telling her to do things, it would have been much easier for her to have given up. The rest you must work out for yourself."

"If you were me, who would you look at closely?"

"Everyone, not especially at the college. I would trust none of your local officers for a start. Look at some of the farmers, or more correctly their outbuildings. And some of their land. Some very odd things get hidden in quarry stores sometimes, you know, explosives. Everyone always thinks quarrymen have the licences for stuff when sometimes they don't or they don't have the right amounts there. Not many people in authority ever check. It would greatly inconvenience them and help us if all explosive places were thoroughly checked. You know I am sure Ruth has quarry friends that she babysits for. I thought the children were grown up. Funny that."

"Oh. I seconded a lass, Sandra Lancashire to the squad. She's local."

"I don't think you need to worry about her. I met her a while ago, no she hasn't been around long enough and I would say is very bright, keen and honest."

"I am curious, do I outrank you?"

"Is that relevant?"

"No, I suppose not, but your reply means that I don't. Don't glare at me like that, I'll cry!"

"The tissues are there. What else do you need to know?"

"You told Nick that you didn't know about the hiding place in the culvert. Did you?"

"I told him that, yes."

"Stop being evasive. That means you knew but didn't want him to know you did. I have never tried to grasp an eel, but I suspect you are a great deal more slippery than a handful of them. I'm not good at milking blood from stones. You still haven't given me a direct answer."

"Someone had to see what was left there, and read the messages that went to and fro. They were very careless. When I looked, no one would ever have known I had."

"Eddie spoke to me on the phone. He said that Grady never acknowledged him, what did he mean?"

"I am sure it would be routine to do DNA tests on victim and killer, would it not? You will work it out."

"They are related?"

She made no reply. She was watching him with a smug smile. She shifted uncomfortably in her seat. She reached into a small bag by her on the table and took a couple of tablets, washed them down with her wine and hopefully held the glass out.

"Are you in pain again, do you want to call it a night? Shall I get you a soft drink, I am sure you should not have too much wine with those tablets."

"Thank you, but if there is any wine left I would rather have that. Then I will sleep well. Something I have not done in months."

Saul opened another bottle and raised his glass to her.

"To a peaceful sleep and to you, madam! You are amazing, annoying, evasive, exasperating and far too clever. Your health, let's carry on can we? Is there any relevance to the far-reaching origins of the students, especially on that course?"

"I think it is always interesting to find out what any local police force knows, don't you? I also think passport control can be very helpful, and immigration. You so often find the unexpected, quite surprising how some things slot together."

"If I turn anything up will it inconvenience you?"

"Not at all. Could be quite helpful. Now Eddie has been caught it would be only natural to investigate anyone on that course. Having a few cages rattled might help me."

"How long do you need to wind your operation up?"

"A couple of months. Maybe sooner. Most of the small players are as good as convicted, we just need to get enough on the bigger fishes in the sewage pond they inhabit, and of course the biggest fish of all. The big event is imminent. We must also protect our friends."

"Is some of it about drugs?"

"Not as such but that is part of it, yes, that's where some of the funding comes from. I let something out about that to you that I shouldn't have done. You will work it out in due course if you haven't already."

"Tilbury?"

"Yes, clever of you. Look I need something from you when the time comes. On a special day, I need to be well out of the way and unobtainable, in a secure place. So, actually, does Nick. There is someone we can't afford to meet in case he clocks us. I therefore need you to get me arrested for something and taken away. I think you will already have done

148

some raids on the college, several I suspect. It is only natural, as you will find a load of drugs in Eddie's locker in the sheep sheds for a start. You might have to do some a couple of days apart so anything found has been replaced, and of course the warrants would have to be for explosives too. When the time comes I think you might have to be on the raid, and take me in."

"For drugs?"

"No that won't work. Everyone knows how anti I am. It will have to be something else, like to prevent a breach of the peace. I can have a row with, say Nick and you could get an officer to hear it and bring us both in. Please, just don't let it be that Celia woman, she might enjoy it a bit too much."

"Oh that will be me, and she wouldn't enjoy it half as much as I will. I wouldn't miss it for the world."

"Then make it realistic because our lives might just depend on it. And those of others."

"Di, you look transparent, tired and I think you are in pain, wouldn't you rather go to bed?"

"I need to let Drift out first. I'll be better when the tablets have kicked in."

"I can do that for you, I've got to let my two out anyway. I have a big garden out there, as you no doubt saw. They can run round for a bit."

"No you won't, not with Drift, she won't go with you yet. She needs to get to know you, I'll come out with you, where did I put that stick?"

They went out to the garden, and watched the dogs disappearing into the darkness.

"I am curious, that syringe you left in the reeds, what was in it, it looked like blood?"

"It was, I had just treated a lamb for a haematoma in the ear. There is a needle there too, a sewing one, with some thread. I had stitched the lamb's ear together with a button to stop it filling up with blood again. It was just as I had done that when Eddie turned up I had to drop it and the crook and take off. There was nowhere to hide so I legged it to the wood. The bullet hit my arm as I swung up into the tree. Eddie wasn't quick enough to get there and couldn't find me and made off when he heard Jim's quad coming. Drift ran off and got into the cave the way I had taught her. The way I got out. Oh, how sweet she has brought me a stick. I just don't have the energy to throw it for you, at the moment, my darling dog."

"No, but I do. Here, fetch!"

Not only did Drift accept Saul as a friend over the next half hour, his own dogs decided having her around made life very interesting. Diana wondered quite what any flower beds would look like in the morning light. As they came back into the house, Anna came in. Saul went to make some cocoa and the three of them sat in the lounge and chatted. Di looked at a picture on the wall and said, "I think you painted this, Mr Catchpole, it is very good; I am impressed."

"To you, in this house, I am Saul, when we are not play-acting for the benefit of others. Yes, it is one of mine. I have to interview Sullivan tomorrow, any suggestions?"

"If you want to really annoy him, ask him about his very slight limp. He has a club foot, that I believe he got from his father, that he won't let anyone see. He is ever so sensitive about it. He flips if anyone calls him Stumpy. I never did but the lads did. He will look for your weakness, and try to use it."

"He already has, he despises the fact I am a Jew. I have never risen to it, and don't intend to start now."

"Are you? That I didn't know."

"I am my family are not. I am not a practising one or devout, Anna is not and I wouldn't impose any religion on anyone, it has to be their own choice."

"How wise. I think I might head up to bed now, the tablets are kicking in, so, I think, is the wine."

Saul got up and helped her up the stairs. At her bedroom door he paused.

"Yes, Saul, you want to ask me something, I think personal. Go ahead."

"You know; from the moment I came up to the farm to talk to you I have had this nagging feeling that we have met before. I have been racking my brains and cannot ever remember anyone with your name, or where or when. Have we met before? I am sure I would remember."

"Oh, yes we have, more than once actually. You know the great thing about being plain, and having very little to distinguish one is that you become totally forgettable. You tend to remember certain things about people, usually something you have in common, like if you have the same colour hair or wear specs or play a certain sport. Maybe you were never told a name, a real name. It will come to you. I was actually helping you then. Goodnight!"

Drift insisted on lying on the bed and early in the morning, Diana got up and quietly let all three dogs out into the garden, where they played very energetically with each other while Di went into the kitchen retrieved her washing from the tumble dryer in the utility room and then made a coffee. When Anna came down she was handed a mug of coffee and then realized the washing up from the previous evening had been done.

"Bless you, I am sure you should still be in bed. I was going to bring you breakfast in bed. You have a bit of colour in your cheeks this morning, are you feeling better?"

"Indeed I am. I had a wonderful night's sleep, for the first time in months I have actually felt safe. I don't want to put you out and would feel awful if you waited on me, I like to be doing! All the dogs have been out, and I gave them some fresh water."

"Yes, where are they, they are suspiciously quiet?"

"In the conservatory, fast asleep. Look, Anna, I am not sure what state the garden is in, they were a bit vigorous last night and this morning. Do you want me to tidy up out there today?"

"No, we don't keep it very tidy. I don't have to go in to work for a couple of days, Saul does. I am just about to do breakfast. The toaster is over there, could you manage to feed it bread? Now would you like eggs and bacon?"

"Bacon, but I thought…"

"Yes, bacon. He won't eat it but I do. I cook it in a separate pan. When he proposed to me I said I wasn't sure I could give up bacon for him. He laughed and said he didn't have a problem with that at all."

"Are your dogs really called Hector and Lysander?"

"Yes. That was Saul's brother's fault, the nice brother that is. I have to go shopping later. Do you want to come? No one will know you. I wondered if you needed anything. I can lend you the money if you don't have any."

"I'd love to come. Is there a cash machine? Jim sent my purse with Drift and a letter saying how worried he had been and wishing me well and that he missed me and the lambs are almost all born now and doing fine. I was due to leave there tomorrow and return to the college next Monday, so it looks like I might only miss a few days. Could I impose for tonight and then I will find somewhere else."

Saul, who had come in, said, "No, we want you to stay with us until you go back to the college. That is at least a week. I would be happier and I am not going to let you out of my sight unless you give me your word you will stop with us. We discussed it, and both agreed."

"If you put it that way, Saul, then thank you, both of you for your kindness and hospitality. It is more than I deserve."

Saul spread a piece of toast with marmalade and took a mouthful out of it.

"Yes, I know. After the way you ran me ragged and the worry you caused, take the advice of your elders and betters and give in gracefully with a bit of dignity."

He was laughing at her and she grinned. She looked him up and down and said, "You know, I might take you seriously if you were not wearing a pair of Lion King slippers and a Formula One dressing gown. Is that a crocodile tooth brush in your hand?"

Anna began to laugh. Saul looked at the two women and said, "I might have known this would happen. Two intelligent women in the house and I am outwitted at the first turn!"

With a broad grin, he retreated upstairs.

Chapter Ten

When Saul had gone off to work, Anna and Di got on really well. They laughed a lot, and both enjoyed each other's company. In the car, on the way to the supermarket, Anna asked, "Tell me if it's none of my business but have you really no family, no one? Or is that what you have to pretend?"

"I had one once, but they were killed. No, I have no one, just Drift. In my line of work, it is better. If something happens, then there is no one left who has to grieve. It is a lonely life. It also means they cannot be used to put pressure on me or as a weapon."

"What do you do at Christmas?"

"Work usually, last Christmas I stayed at college and helped with the stock."

"We always have friends round. We do celebrate it, Saul just doesn't go to church with us. He occasionally takes himself off to the synagogue in town. Will you come to us this year?"

"If I am still around, I should love to."

"I hope you get paid a great deal for what you do. There must be some rewards to make you do it."

"Yes, I can have pretty much what I want. I am actually quite well off in my own right. I earn a great deal. I do it for another reason."

"Can I ask what that is?"

"I suppose it could best be described as a sort of patriotism. There are not many of us you know. I get something out of it, knowing I have done the right thing. When everything I held dear was destroyed around me, I decided I could only deal with it if I devoted myself to stopping that kind of thing in a small way. I made the decision years ago and it has become my life. Makes me a boring fart, I know. I have never really tried to rationalize it. It would hurt too much. Not everyone is destined to have a happy family life. At least what I do makes more people able to. I have moments of great excitement, great fear, pain, and hardship, but I also get experiences most people would never even think possible. Each job is so different, and a new challenge. I don't always succeed, but my record isn't bad. I think I have spent so long being someone else that I don't really know who I am any more. There are good times. Can we leave it, it hurts a bit to explain and you are about the first person I have ever said this to?"

"Would you rather I didn't tell Saul any of this?"

"No, not at all. I think he is struggling to work out what I am about. I told him, once, years ago, about what people like me do, and how they must remain, detached. I think he was the only one of them, on that course, that even had a slight inkling that people like me existed."

"You do know you are driving him to distraction trying to remember when you met? He had a nightmare last night, and woke up saying, 'But she had red hair too'."

"I didn't mean to do that. Could you suggest to him that years ago, just before he went on his spell in Special Branch, he went on a surveillance course at Hendon? Later he went on an intelligence course there too. There were officers from all over the country. They never were told the real names of the instructors, each had a code name. It is very seldom I meet anyone with his sensitivity and brains, and I am afraid I rather enjoy the occasional mind game. I am sorry, I will try to stop it. There are things I can't tell him, you realize that?"

"Please don't stop. He has sort of woken up, and he is rather enjoying the challenge I think. You are very, very senior aren't you? He is wondering how senior."

"Yes, very. It scares most senior officers, they like to feel they are in charge. It isn't a thing I consider much, unless I have to use it, which isn't often. Is this the store, great, I can have a wonderful time spending. I don't get to do it too often, you see a student at an agricultural college doesn't have a lot of money or expensive things. I get bored of just being what I am all the time. Let's go spend some of my money!"

*

Saul spent an hour reading paperwork before meeting Celia and interviewing Eddie. It was an introductory interview, and lasted only a few minutes as Eddie refused to say anything at all. They put him back in the cell, and then Saul went back to his office and listened to the tape of his interview with Diana again, and one or two other tapes. He managed two coffees during this time and after a trip to the bathroom, he returned to his office to find his Chief Constable and two strange men in his office.

The Chief shut the door and said, "Saul, I think you know who Mr Jones and Mr Smith really are. They have told me what I need to know. Please, talk to them. I will be in my office if you need me. I don't need to hear the details. Thank you, gentlemen. Saul, come to me for the necessary authorities and for what you need."

As the Chief left the room he slid the engaged sign onto the door.

Later, Saul found Celia and once again they went to interview Eddie, who refused a solicitor with a disparaging laugh, and said he had nothing to say.

Saul said, "Fair enough, but we are entitled to find out your identity. What is your real name? You have several passports in your possession. What other names are you known by, other than Stumpy?"

Eddie flipped. He sprang from his seat, and attacked Saul trying to strangle him, and was pulled off by two very large and strong custody officers who had been asked to be present. Eddie screamed, "I'm not called that! If anyone calls me that, I'll kill them. Mike called me that. Even my mother did. She paid for it too, what she did to me. She never wanted me. The kids at school called me that once. I soon got them back. It isn't wise to cross me you know. You'll find out. Something nasty will happen to you, it always does. I'm special, chosen you know. You can't stop me."

"Do tell me, how are you going to do that from the confines of a cell?"

"I'll be out of here before you know it. I have friends, they'll get me out. I'm far too important to be kept in here. You don't even know who you are talking to, do you?"

"That is what I am trying to ascertain. Exactly who are you?"

"I don't want to speak to you any more. I want to go back to my cell."

As they left the cell block, Saul chuckled and said, "That worked well. Now I know where to start looking."

Celia said, "It did? I've been through all the paperwork and nowhere does it refer to him as Stumpy. How did you think that one up?"

"I was told. Please run a search under that nickname or alias. With the Garda too. I think our violent friend might have ·been on a violent path for many years. It might give us a starting point. Also look up under Murphy and Grady and O'Grady if you have not already done so. Young Nita can help you. I am afraid, Celia, you will have to accept that I am privy to information that you might not have and that you are not security cleared to have. I will give you what I can."

"That woman Green told you didn't she? You know she has disappeared off the face of the earth? I had a DCI asking me if I knew where she was, apparently there is a warrant out for her for a burglary. He asked me if I knew where she was, and to help track her down. Do you know where she is?"

"Yes I do. No, I will not tell you. Who was this DCI? Just remember, you are working for me, not him. You are pushing your luck, madam, just at the moment. Get it into your head, Green is not a murder suspect, she is a vital witness. Do not discuss anything we are dealing with, with anyone not on the squad. You are excellent at organizing things, logistics and I value you, but just back off!"

"DCI Thornaby, sir. Oh God, I have got it all wrong haven't I? It was just that, well, I was told she wasn't what she portrayed to be, early on, and that I shouldn't trust her. I thought I was doing the right thing and that you were taken in by her, I am sorry. Geoff told me I need to apologize to you, and I was being stupid. I have been, haven't I? I am so, so sorry."

"Apology accepted. Yes you have, but it has only made life harder for you. Do you think I don't know the squad have been giving you the cold shoulder? No more than you deserve. I will put that right, but I want you to succeed, Celia. In many ways you are a fine officer with a good career in front of you. I will give you some advice, though, which you would do well to take on board. After any confrontation, or operation, ask if anyone is hurt or needs help. Officers will admire you for it. Even if you don't care, pretend you do. The officers around you may one day save your life, remember that. Who told you about Green, early on, and when?"

"Thornaby. I used to work with him a few years back, when I was a detective constable. He rang me just before we went out to interview her."

"Who did you tell we were going there?"

"I can't remember, oh yes, WPC Makin, when I was in the toilets before we left. I know her too, she works with Thornaby now, I believe. She asked me where I was off to. I got the call from Thornaby shortly afterwards, while I was filling the car up."

"Did you not think their interest a little strange? You do not discuss the squad business with anyone at all, do you understand? I will tell you now, I have had several calls from friends to tell me you are not trustworthy any more, I will sort that, but be very careful. Just now, the Chief asked me if I wanted him to take you off the squad, which I am afraid would be the end of, or seriously delay, your promotion chances in CID. I said no, I needed you. You are very much on probation, so don't let me down again! Now let's go and have a cup of coffee in the canteen. You need everyone to see we are still the best of friends. You are buying and I will have a flapjack and an iced bun. So will you, you have gone as white as a sheet. I seem to be spending a lot of time looking after the health of women these days. Come on, it can be fixed you know."

"Did Sullivan hurt you, when he had a go? I never thought to ask, and I should have tried to stop him I suppose, but I thought the two custody officers could cope."

"Not really, but thanks for asking. I am glad you didn't get hurt, and also I doubt you could have helped a lot, he is very strong, and you are not. When did you have your last fitness test? Next time he is interviewed he will be in restraints."

"I ducked the last two, I am afraid, I hate physical exercise."

"Yes I know you did, I do get told these things, I will leave the solution for that to you. Let's take the stairs up to the canteen, not the lift, and I will race you. Go!"

In the squad office a couple of hours later, Celia knew things had altered when she was offered a digestive biscuit with her coffee. Suddenly the atmosphere had changed and when Geoff walked by, he winked at her. She knew she had been given another chance.

Later, Saul called her into his office, shut the door and motioned her to sit down. He smiled and said, "I need your help, Celia. You must realize that this isn't just about the murders any more. We have another bigger problem to work on. As soon as we have finished talking I want you to go away, somewhere on your own and read this file, all of it. Don't let anyone see it or you reading it. Bring it straight back to me. Now, what is your opinion of young Nita, helping in the office here? I think you are due to do an appraisal on her very soon."

"Yes, she has been such a help, she is very efficient. She is not CID as such is she? She is on light duties officially but she works harder than most. She is not allowed on outside enquiries, that I do know. I should know more about the staff working for me, shouldn't I?"

"Yes. She is very bright. She was in despair when she thought she would have to be medically discharged after an accident, a car crash. Her supervisor came to see me about her. He said she was too valuable to lose. I want you to make a lot of enquiries through her and on your own, discreet ones, Nita is good at them. I want to know who would have taken on these murder enquiries if I hadn't been available and able to do so. You may need to talk to British transport about it. Tell them as little as you can, and when you have found who to talk to, get them to call or come and see me.

Next I need some heavy research into backgrounds, all on this list. As you see it is highly confidential, and no one outside you, me, Geoff and Nita must know. I have arranged for two isolated offices with a couple of secure telephone lines just down the corridor. Locked offices with coded access. You will need to contact Special Branch, Immigration, The FBI, The DEA, the Royal Canadian Mounted Police, as well as the RUC, and the Garda. I have written a couple of contacts I have down, that I trust. Also the Sûreté. If you need to visit abroad, which you may well need to do, I trust you have a current passport. I need checks done with the Yard and get any DNA profile details, if available, to compare against any we have. These two names you will not make any reference to or enquiries about, yes Nick and Diana. Here is the authority to do all this, that is what you quote and the codes you use. Please learn them by heart and hand that paper back to me, and do not copy it. Tell no one else except Nita, and Geoff, and we will have to get a bit more help. I will pick them if you don't mind. That is my next task."

"You are trusting me with this after what I have done?"

"Yes. That is past, and I doubt you will make the same mistakes again, but I will ask you, are you prepared to do it? It might just be dangerous. We are dealing with some powerful enemies. If you are, then it will not do your promotion chances any harm, if we get it right. I will not hold it against you if you don't want to. It has to be a free choice that you, and you alone, make now. I will tell you I think you will do it better than I could, you have that kind of analytical mind. Your personnel records say you can speak French is that so? You can say nothing else to anyone about this conversation, I shall deny it if you ever refer to it if you say no. I would tell you to stop crying on me but the last time I said anything like that, the woman nearly died on me, and I got covered in blood. The suit has had to be dry cleaned, twice. Why the tears? Here, tissues."

"The answer is yes, I do want to do it. I have spent the last couple of hours wondering if I had any police career left, and wondering if I was in the right job. I have been so self-centred and selfish, and I have just been given the most exciting challenge I will ever have, by you, whom I let down so badly. Thank you, thank you, thank you!"

"Oh don't over-dramatize things! Let's get on. When you have read that, there is another list, yes of course write it down, just incinerate what you record at the end of the day and show it to nobody. Find out from the college where Eddie did any attachments and where he was known to visit, go, shop, sell drugs, drink, everything you can. The same for Ruth, Alison, Haggis and Steve. Then get the dog section in to search any and all farms that Eddie had any contact with. Drugs and explosives and money is what we are looking for. That might be a good training exercise I think. If any farmers don't want to, let me know. I want you to get Callum to help you. He won't ask why, he knows better. He is just due to be promoted, by the way, and is joining the squad as Inspector until his new posting comes through. Take his advice, and do kit yourself out with some outdoor clothes. If you can't afford them I will pay for them.

Next we will be doing a huge drugs search of the college, all of it. It might take a couple of days. We will start in the sheep unit, and then get the working animal areas cleared as soon as we can. I do have a warrant but Hardaker has also given written permission, for everything. He has the authority for every building on the campus. I want him with you, as the raid progresses. Don't let him out of your sight. I think he is safe but I cannot be sure. OK? I will give you further detail nearer the time, and I want a list of officers who are due to do it. There may be some I don't want, or to know about it in advance. Then two days later we will go in again and re-search. We will have found drugs on the first raid, I am reliably informed and this time no one will know until we get there. Don't worry, I have the chief's backing and the budget. We will also be checking parts of the railway line, and I will have the Transport man with me on that."

"Did I just agree to doing all this? We are going to need more than Nita to help me. Can we second anyone, maybe a couple of local CID?"

"Definitely not them. Please listen, there are very few local officers we can trust. I will find us someone. Tell no one. I do not want divisional commanders told, and the chief backs me on that."

"That sounds ominous. Rather scary!"

"Yes it is."

"Will we be using the drug squad?"

"Not ours, no, another one, from a different force. On your way out, can you get Nita in to see me?"

"Sure, sir, I think you should know another person wanted to know where Diana has gone."

"Who?"

"A DC Simon Alder, from Lorraine's patch. I met him in the corridor, yesterday. He wanted to know what the squad was doing and what it was about and how things were going. I thought he was just being curious. No one in the canteen could talk about much else after Eddie was arrested."

"I'll bet! That was a good job, well done. Why didn't you ring me, and leave it to Terry?"

"I was being pig-headed and was in a strop about what Geoff had said. I told Alder I didn't know and hadn't time to gossip about it."

At tea time, when a lot of officers and headquarters staff were there for the afternoon break, Saul took himself into the canteen. He looked round and was conscious of a sudden hush while everyone wondered why he was there. A couple of officers got up, and offered him their seat in the crowded canteen, which he politely declined, thanking them for their civility and respect. He spotted a long-standing friend, and walked up to him, took him gently by the arm and said, "Wally, I need your help. Can you come and see me in the store just down from the collator's office, in a couple of minutes?"

Saul left the canteen, very aware of a strange silence at his unpredictable behaviour. Wally, a senior officer of many years' standing, said, "As you were, everyone! Don't you have work to get back to?"

Wally followed Saul and they closed the door of the store and walked to the back of it out of any possible earshot.

"Saul, really, what are you up to? Now you have given the whole building something to wonder at. What do you want?"

"You are not from the divisions I am working in. Can you recommend two straight, trustworthy officers or civilians who I can borrow to do some secret and vitally important inside work in a squad office for a couple of months. I need someone from outside my area. Someone who can keep their mouth shut."

"What kind of enquiries?"

"Liaising with other agencies personnel research, preferably HOLMES trained though that is not essential. For a good reason I don't want to go through personnel department."

"Hang on, let me think, I gather I don't want to know why. I can think of one straight away. He is office bound, he has early MS and is just hanging on for his pension. You might know him, good chap, Fred Dunlop. There is a young WPC, pregnant but very capable, no that's not how I meant to put that, I mean, she is capable and also happens to be pregnant. She has a couple of months to go before going on maternity leave, before she has the baby. I was wondering where to put her. She lives not far from here. Her husband is not in the job, works on the oil rigs I think. I would trust them both."

"Thanks, yes I know Fred Dunlop, he would do very well. What is her name?

"Lauren Bakeup."

"I don't know her. It is pretty urgent."

"I will get them both to report to you now shall I?"

"Can you?"

"At my rank, I hope so. How are you keeping, anyway? Leg better now, you over-brave impetuous fool? Healed I hope. Not seen you for an age. I am up here on a course. We both know what a bore some can be. I think we first met on one didn't we?"

Saul froze and then stared at Wally, until Wally started to look nervously around to see what he was staring at.

"You all right, man? Have I grown a second nose? Saul, snap out of it, you are worrying me!"

"Hunter, of course! Sorry, Wally, but you just gave me the answer to a problem I have had for days now. Thank you, my friend, how is Gwen? I trust you are in good health?"

"Yes we're fine. I'll catch up with you another time, but you get back to your secret playtime, go on, Bye! I'll send them up to you, they are both on duty today."

Celia opened the inquest on Grady that afternoon, and Eddie was remanded in custody by video link from the high-security wing of a prison just outside York. Returning from court Celia felt so lucky, Saul had put her down as the officer in the case and she reflected it would do her promotion chances a lot of good. Somehow her personal life had pushed her dedication and judgement rather out of place. She vowed she would never let it happen again. She called in at a sports shop on the way back to the office and got some running shoes and a tracksuit and a couple of tee shirts. As she came back into the main entrance of the headquarters she went to take the lift and then changed her mind, and headed for the stairs instead. It occurred to her that Saul seldom if ever took the lift, using the stairs. She still knew very little about him. Obviously he kept fit, and knew a lot about everyone who he worked with. It was an example for her to follow. She would buy some outdoor clothes on her next day off. As she climbed breathlessly up the third flight of steps and turned the corner for the fourth Saul was there talking to one of the cleaners. Saul looked at her bags, and grinned and peeled off to join her.

"I am impressed, Celia, well done. Our extra help is just about to arrive. I will need you to help brief them and get them an office space, in the new offices, of course, I've just fixed up with housekeeping about the cleaning arrangements, in other words we do it, as no one else will be allowed in. Do you want help with those bags?"

"Thanks, but how will I get fit if I don't do it myself, I can hardly keep up with you as it is."

Being a gentleman, Saul slowed down and kept pace with her back to their offices. She had just got her breath back when Saul beckoned her down to the new offices where Nita was already busy. Two strangers came in and they all sat down, after Saul had pointedly secured the door.

"Hello, Fred, it is good to see you. You must be Lauren, this is Nita Patel and this is DI Celia Allenby. I am Detective Chief Superintendent Saul Catchpole. From this time on we do not worry much about rank, I am therefore Saul to all of you. Thanks for coming in at such short notice. This job requires total secrecy. That means from any other officers, even on my murder squad, unless I tell you otherwise with the exception of Sergeant Geoff Bickerstaff. If there is a leak, my head will roll and yours too. This office and the one next door will be alarmed by the time I leave tonight. You will each have your own access code and will tell only those here now what they are. This is not a public office even to senior officers no matter where they are from or how senior they are, up to the rank of Deputy Chief Constable. The Chief can come in, he will have his own code. If you are ordered to open up, you have an overriding one from the Chief, and you can tell whoever tries that I will be informed immediately, which I would expect to be, wherever I am."

"Now, you will undoubtedly be the most popular people in the canteen, tell them absolutely nothing except that this is Operation Moon. We are investigating someone called Hunter.

It is a complicated bank fraud involving currencies. We aren't but that is what you say if anyone presses you, and you tell me who does. Be wary of invitations and if anything unusual occurs seek company and help. When you go tonight you will get your security passes. You will work what hours you want, flexible to get the job done, and I insist you keep all medical appointments you have, I will authorize overtime if Celia can't. Yes, Fred?"

"Are we in uniform?"

"No. I don't care what you wear, well, something preferably, bikini and a kilt if you must. I need you comfortable. I see you have already acquired a kettle and fridge, I have no idea how, Nita, but I think it might be easier to have coffee breaks and the like here. Here is some money for tea coffee and milk. I will try convince my wife she has too many mugs and bring some in."

"Don't bother, Saul, I have loads and plates and cutlery. I'll bring them in tomorrow."

"Thanks, Fred."

"No rubbish goes out and you burn anything unwanted in the incinerator downstairs, personally. Work out a rota between you, and let me have a copy. Fred, will you act up? Good. There may be some risk to you, I won't try to deny it. We need a signal, so we know someone is in trouble, a code word or sign, any ideas?"

"We are supposed to be doing currency? Why don't we use the Indonesian one, Bahts, it should be easy to include in a sentence? He is bats, or are you bats, or cricket bats, without being too obvious."

"That is brilliant, thank you, Lauren, I think I have some at home and we can each have our own denomination, if you leave it on the desk we will come and find you. Three murders have already been committed in this affair and I don't want any more."

*

When Saul got home about nine that evening, he found Anna and Di in fits of laughter, in the kitchen, with a meal having been prepared by them. They had been having fun cooking together and were, he suspected, moderately drunk. The three dogs were lying comatose in the conservatory. When he went to kiss Anna on the cheek, she said, "I wish you would bring me company like this more often, darling. I haven't laughed this much for years. Now sit down and we will serve you a banquet. Di has knackered the dogs in the park, and even weeded some of the garden before I could stop her, and she found and fixed the squeak in the door of my car. Please get her to rest, I can't."

"I see. Well, Mrs Hunter, be warned I will cart you back to the hospital if you don't. I had a visit today, from your colleagues. We need to talk more."

"I know, they told me. You have worked it out, I knew you would. Clever of you, it was a long time ago. This is the first time I have felt safe for ages and it has done me a power of good."

"I am delighted to hear it. Thank you for what you have done here. Do I get a wine too?"

The women began to giggle and Saul looked in the bin and sighed and went over to the wine rack to get another. The rack was full and he took out a bottle and said, "This is a really good bottle of wine, and so is this, and this. Anna, where did you get them? They are way beyond our budget."

"I didn't, Di did. She insisted it was in lieu of rent. We just had to try a bottle, there was no room for it in the rack."

Saul looked in a bag beside the rack and saw at least another dozen bottles waiting to be put away. In the bin there was another empty bottle.

"Just the one was it? Really, ladies, you *are* drunk!"

"I might be but Di isn't. It doesn't seem to affect her at all."

As Saul opened the next bottle he looked again at the label.

"Where did you learn so much about wine?"

"I had to be employed at a wine merchants for a while. I learned very quickly. The expert who taught me was very knowledgeable I was quite upset when he went away, but there was nothing I could do about it."

"Were you also a gardener?"

"Yes it was another job I had. I spent a while in a massive gardens and became rather an expert on orchids and when I finally settle down I would like to grow them. There is a lot of money in orchids you know. I found a rare one today at the garden centre. It is in the conservatory now. I hoped you would give it a home."

Saul went into the conservatory stepping over three sleeping and snoring dogs, and looked at the plant, and came back and said, "I have never seen one so large or so beautiful. The scent is divine. When you are settled you can have it back."

"No, I'll get another. Keep it."

After their meal, they went into the lounge and Saul asked Anna, "Where is the foreign currency pot, I need it?"

"In the drawer of the desk, second one down. Di, tell me the rest of that joke about the lambs."

Saul spread the notes out on the table and selected those he wanted. Di glanced over and said, "When did you go to Thailand? I always rather liked the idea of dealing in Bahts. It rather appealed to my sense of humour. I had visions of vampire bats being the high denominations and fruit bats the lower ones. Did you know that here in this country we have pipistrelle bats? I recently found out there are soprano pipistrelle bats too. I had visions of a choir of upside down bats, you know, bass bats, tenor bats and alto bats, all being conducted by a horseshoe bat."

Anna laughed.

"We went last year when Saul was convalescing. When were you there?"

"A couple of years ago, I was working with orchids there. I had to help on an orchid hunt. I loved the wildlife. I had work to do, but the most exciting thing was when a man was bitten by a snake. I had to act really quickly and saved him. He did recover but I don't think I did him much of a favour, he won't be going anywhere ever again. Did you want to talk again, Saul?"

Anna got up.

"I'm off to have a bath, and I will leave you two super sleuths to talk. I don't want to know anything about it."

Saul sat down in an easy chair and said, "You look much better. Just how long have you been doing this work, Di?"

172

"A long time, it takes its toll. I always hope that this one is the last, but it never is."

"You lost your family through it?"

"What family I had yes. Tony and I worked as a pair. He was killed. It broke my heart. I vowed to carry on until I could do no more, but that time is coming soon I think."

"Why did they choose you for this one?"

"They didn't. I did. Right background, my way with animals. Right motivation, right time, right direction."

They talked for some time, and then Di said, "I'll take the dogs out in the garden for their last visit. You have a lovely family, Saul, thanks for your kindness. I met your son, Sam today. I don't want to intrude."

"Did he have his lady friend with him?"

"Tatum, yes I liked her and I think he is great. He looks very like you did when you were a fair bit younger, when I knew you. I went out into the garden and left them with Anna. I needed some thinking time. Drift, Hector, Lysander, wake up, you lazy hounds, time to go out."

Chapter Eleven

The next Sunday, Saul only had to go into work for a couple of hours, and was home in time for Sunday lunch. The family had come for the day and went and sat in the lounge, Saul missed Diana and went into the kitchen to find her just finishing the washing up and tidying.

"You are not intruding. Come back and join us?"

"Thanks, but I've been so isolated upon the farm lots of people make me edgy. Can I take the dogs up the park? I need the exercise. You go and relax with your family. Anna is already asleep. I could do with some time out and I have a couple of calls to make."

"If that suits you, of course. If you are not back in, say, an hour, I'll come and find you. I need you to get well, not suffer in silence, as you have been doing. I found out exactly what your injuries were and stop trying to pretend they are mere scratches. How are your feet now?"

"Healing well, how am I going to get my car back from Moorside Farm? And the few things I left there like my tools?"

"I got them all fetched for you and they are locked in a spare locker at HQ. Your car is in a lockup garage. Donald sent this for you."

"Oh, my wages, thanks. I'll be back in a couple of hours. I have my phone if I need anything."

"Take care of yourself."

When Saul realized the family were all asleep in front of a very boring film, he got his coat and as it was time for her to return, decided to go and meet her. He got to the entrance of the park, by an old lodge and was passing the trees there when he saw the dogs. Then he saw two uniformed police officers talking to Diana beside a small potting shed. The dogs were sitting firmly and resolutely between the officers and her, and he could hear Drift growling softly. He slunk round the back of the buildings and listened. One of the men said, "If you have no identification, and no good reason for being here then until we have established who you are, I will detain you. Where are you staying?"

"Do you know I don't actually know the address, how silly of me! I'm just visiting. My friends popped in to see a relative of theirs who is poorly, and I was obviously in the way, so I came out with the dogs, found this lovely park, and then you came."

"Who are these friends?"

"John and Jane McKenzie. They live up at Conistone, near Grassington. You see, I had an accident recently, and they asked if I wanted to come for a drive, as I have been laid up. Whatever have I done wrong, officer?"

"It is an offence to have a dog in a public place without a name and address on its collar. One of your dogs doesn't even have a collar and the other two have no identification. Now, tell me exactly who you are."

"My name is Georgina Boddington."

"Have you a middle name?"

"Yes, Rachel. I am staying at six Wood Lane Kilnsey. I have no idea what the post code is. These Labradors belong to my friends. The collie is my dog, you see I am a shepherd, and had an accident. I didn't think a working dog had to have a collar."

"It does here, in this city. Where are you a shepherd then and who is your employer?"

"A Douglas Russel, and he lives at Ebbor Farm, Ebbor Gorge, Near Wells. I live in the farm cottage there."

"You look a lot like this woman in this photograph here, who is a Diana Green".

"My goodness, I do don't I? How strange but I don't know anyone of that name. I can assure you that is not me. She looks a bit scruffy, don't you think?"

"Well, I think it is you and there is a warrant out for you for burglary. I am arresting you. Walk towards the car please."

Saul had to admire how Diana could burst into tears and come over as a simple and innocent rather silly woman. He decided the matter had gone far enough. He walked up to the three of them and it was obvious that they knew who he was, as they looked nervously at each other. Saul prayed the dogs wouldn't give him away.

"Good afternoon, officers, is everything all right?"

"Just checking this woman, sir. She answers the description of someone wanted for burglary. We were asked to look in this area."

"Who by? I know of no such warrant, just check on your radio with the CRO office please. May I see that photo you have?"

He held his hand out rather imperiously and was handed the photograph. It was not one issued by any police organization. He hoped they had not noticed that Drift had stopped growling and his two dogs were wagging their tails.

"Well, I suppose we could. DCI Thornaby briefed us special on parade today."

"Did he now? Let's just check it with control room shall we?"

As one of them called up on his radio, Saul turned to Diana and asked, "What are you doing here?"

"Just walking the dogs, who are you?"

He showed her his warrant card and made a point of showing it to one of the officers as well.

"I am a rather senior police officer. You don't look much like a burglar to me, are you one? How did you get all those bandages?"

"I had an accident on the farm where I work in Somerset. The quad bike's brakes failed and I was thrown some way. What does a burglar look like? I wouldn't know. I've never seen one I don't think. My boss sent me up here for a holiday. I do wish they could ring him and he will tell you who I am."

"Give me the number, and I will ring him now."

The embarrassment of the two officers was quite obvious when the checks confirmed that no such warrant existed and no one called Diana Green was wanted or known for anything, was rather gratifying. It was enhanced when Lord Douglas Russel not only described her dog, and her and confirmed everything she said. He had asked after her and hoped the officers were assisting her. The two constables apologised and Saul pointedly asked if Diana needed a lift anywhere. She said her friends were picking her up in about ten minutes. Saul looked at the two men and said, "Tell me did you check the warrant existed? No, I didn't think so. I will sign your pocket books now, please."

He looked at the books, and pointedly signed, dated and timed them and said, "You have a bit of explaining to do, both of you. Not now, not here. I advise you to get out of my sight right now."

He turned to Diana and said, "I am so sorry, Mrs Boddington, for this incident. Do you wish to make a formal complaint? No, how generous of you. May I offer you assistance of any kind? Will you accept I shall follow this up? Let me wait with you at the gate until your friends arrive."

When the police car had driven off Saul said, "Can you get back home? I'm going to wait here and see who turns up. I'll be back soon. Oh, boy, am I going to enjoy carpeting them! I'll explain later. Go in the back way and make sure you are not seen. The dogs will show you the side alley leading to the back gate. The code on the lock is 1212."

"Not Whitehall first? OK, ta."

He waited by the gate well out of sight while she walked off with the dogs. About ten minutes later, a car drew up and so did the police vehicle from earlier. He saw Thornaby get out and look round, and the two constables joined him.

"You are sure it was her?"

"We thought so, guv. It looked like her. She had a white-faced collie too, like the one in the background of that picture. It came back as no trace, I don't understand."

"It must be an admin error, I'll sort it out. I'll see him and smooth the way for you. If you see her again, just watch and see where she goes. Now go back to your duties. I'll see you right, don't worry. It is what I am paying you for."

The police car drove off and Thornaby got out his mobile phone and rang someone.

"They are sure it was her, but it went wrong. Carrot Top happened along and sent them off with a flea in their ears. I'll keep trying to find her. Yes, he will believe me he always has before. Yes, more fool him, bye."

Saul watched him drive off, making a mental note of the car and its number. He walked smartly home. He had never really taken to Thornaby and now he knew why. Once home he recorded everything in his pocket book and went and found Diana, who was grooming Drift. From the smart appearance of his two she had already done them. Both of them had got the tags on their collars, and he noticed Drift had her usual quite substantial collar on. He wondered why it had never seemed a little odd before that a working dog would have such a collar.

She looked up and smiled and he said, "How the hell did you stop the dogs from giving it away?"

"I asked them not to. Are they real officers? I didn't like them much?"

"Yes they are. Deeply in the shit now. One hadn't made his pocket book up for over two weeks and the other was longer. Signs of a sloppy supervisor, that. How did you get the dog tags off so quick?"

"I saw them look at me and when they drove past a second time and then returned and came back I decided I didn't want them connecting me with you. They are not a good advertisement for the force, Saul. They were aggressive and ignorant. Their knowledge of law is very wanting. I know of no 'city' law here about dog collars."

"Neither do I, and there isn't one. Is this Lord Russel real?"

"Totally, so is Georgina Boddington. She has a dog exactly like mine. We have the same line of work. Is there a warrant?"

"No. Here, this photo, how did they get that do you think?"

She looked at it and sat down and then stared into the middle distance for a couple of minutes and then looked at the photo again.

"This is worrying, I know who took that, and when. It was Mike. I asked him to delete it and he said he had. I hate having my photo taken. It was at the beginning of the course. I think it is obvious that they now know that I am a threat to them or I am involved in this. I need to make some calls. Here, have it back, I don't want it, bin it. What are you going to do? You are pretty angry about this, I think."

"I might just have time to inspect the whole shift. Will you be all right here?"

"Fine, I won't go further than the garden. Thanks for rescuing me. Have fun!"

"Oh, I will. I'll see you when I get back."

Saul, accompanied by an inspector and several others from Complaints and Discipline swept into the small station thirty minutes before the shift was due to book off. They went straight to the canteen where seven male officers were playing cards. There was a pot of money on the table in front of them and the ashtrays were full. The place reeked of tobacco smoke. An inspector walked in from the adjoining rest room where it appeared he had been asleep. The officers stared blankly at them until one realized who they were, sprang to his feet and commanded, "Attention!"

Slowly the others got to their feet.

"Thank you. I am Detective Chief Superintendent Catchpole and this is Inspector Collingwood from Complaints and Discipline. I want all your pocket books now, yours too, Inspector Smith. Where are the other members of the shift?"

"I don't know, sir, dealing with an accident on the Harrogate road."

"What time was that?"

"About half eight, sir."

"Sergeant, you are their direct supervisor, you should know. I will point out that gambling is not permitted on police premises, and neither is smoking unless in a designated area which this is not. Just what have you lot done in the last three hours?"

"I went on an alarm call about nine, and PC Oxted is writing up a sudden-death report from this afternoon, until about ten minutes ago."

"And the rest of you?"

"We just came in from foot patrol, sir, me and Jack."

"No you didn't. We've been sat watching this station for the last four hours. Falsehood is a disciplinary offence as you well know. Are any of these books up to date, Malcolm?"

"Only one, sir. You seem to have had a busy day, PC Oxted. The rest are so out of date as to be worthy of action. PC Oxted, as soon as your relief comes on you are excused. The rest of you remain in this room. Inspector, Sergeant, downstairs with me now!"

The two officers he had met earlier that evening were found in an office in the cell block frantically writing up their pocket books. A little later the three women officers on the shift came in, having dealt with most of the calls for the whole shift. Their books were up to date. Saul left the matter with the appropriate department and returned home, where he found Diana had gone to bed and his wife was just about to. He had a shower and joined her.

Chapter Twelve

Nick Greenwood was enjoying the half hour he had to relax, with his dogs. The early morning chores had been completed by the duty students and the sheep were in the handling pens waiting for the first session of the day, when the remains of the sheep course were returning from holiday to dose the sheep. They were mostly quite able now, and he could rely on them to do a good job.

Janet, as usual, had come down to the pens early, and was working the training sheep in the small field nearby with her dog, Bet. He put his dogs in the kennels and went to watch her. She called her dog back after a while and came over to him.

"So, how did your lambing go?"

"Hard work but I think I did all right. What has been going on here, Nick? Where is Diana? Is it true that Eddie was arrested?"

"Yes. Diana got hurt and went to hospital. Did the coppers come and talk to you?"

"Yes, they told me Mike had been killed. It must have been horrid for all of you. When I was in the bar last night, no one could talk about anything else. Do you know what really happened?"

"Some of it, Eddie killed Mike, so they say, over in Pump House field. We have had the police swarming all over the place for a week or more. If you know anything tell them, would you do me a favour?"

"What?"

"Could you look after Eddie's dog until we sort out what to do with it? I think Diana wants to buy it, if not I shall have to find another owner."

"Yes all right, I wouldn't mind having him, I got offered a permanent job on my last farm."

"You must have impressed them. Go for it."

"What are we going to do now Mike isn't here?"

"The other tutors will take over. One does your shearing anyway. Incidentally all your marks have been reassessed. I think you will be pleased. Hardaker came down and told me. You are top of the class!"

"That is a relief. Diana will have the best theory marks and assignment marks."

"And you have the best practical ones. Keep it up. Here come the others, we had better get started. What the hell, Diana is here! I was told she would be laid up for a while. She can hardly dose sheep with her arm in bandages. I'll get her to bring the next lot of sheep. Will you go with her? Your two dogs can cope easily. Bring them down from Twelve Acre field please, and get the Suffolks in for me please and put them in the outer pens."

Janet walked off with Diana and on their way down to the far fields, they talked.

"Should you be here?"

"Yes I can't sit on my bum all day. It will be a relief to get back to simple sheep work, I've had a bit too much of an exciting time. First I get suspected of murder and then I get shot at. Not nice at all. How are things with you?"

They chatted amiably for an hour while the Suffolks were rounded up and on the way back down the drive Janet said, "Do you want Biff, Eddie's dog? If not, I will buy him. I will need another."

"Then take him. I doubt I shall have the work for two, not for a while anyway. I am so pleased about you getting that job, well done! You deserve it."

"And you deserve a bloody medal after what you did for Zoe, which you have rather neglected to mention. You are not quite what you seem, are you? Will I ever see you again, after this course is over?"

"I hope so. Janet, could you keep thoughts like that to yourself please. I am just another student. I have no wish to stand out as anything else. Hell, why do Suffolks always have to go in the wrong direction? I'll get them back. We don't want them lumbering around the car park. Drift, cum bye!"

"Because they are thick. Bet, away, away!

*

At headquarters, Saul was meeting with a visiting Garda officer. They were joined by several other interesting and high-ranking officials from several countries and agencies. As they moved to the senior officers' conference room, they were passed by Thornaby, who said, "Sir, I wanted a chat with you.

I think there has been a mix-up over a warrant I thought existed. Can I see you now?"

"I am busy at the moment, Roger, I'll get back to you."

"I can wait in your office, if you like."

"No, I'll be a while, I think, I'll call you."

Once they lost sight of him, Saul said, "Bother. Do any of you know him or he you?"

"I met him last year when we did that raid on illegal immigrants on that farm."

"What does he know about you?"

"Just that I am from immigration, I didn't have a lot to do with him, I didn't like him much."

"Nor do I!"

The meeting was highly productive and some good plans were made. Back in the Operation Moon offices, Nita put the kettle on and said to Saul, "Thanks for inviting us three along, sir. I, for one felt very privileged at being there. I did like that CIA man, Dwight whatever his name was. He was like a squash ball on heat! I like the Frenchman, from the Gendarme too."

"Yes and I am grateful for your considerable linguistic abilities, Nita, I didn't know your French was that good. I am very impressed. Fred, you obviously get by in German. My French is very limited. I do speak Yiddish but that wasn't much help there! Thanks, everyone."

Lauren came back into the room.

"I am sorry, the trouble with being pregnant is having to use the loo so often. Who has been trying to get into the office while we were in that meeting? The pad on the other door is flashing."

"Is it?"

Saul got up and went and had a look and reset the pad. As the alarm had not gone off no one had got in, but several different numbers had been keyed into the pad, including all their warrant numbers and their pay code numbers. Once back in the office he said, "I think this was inevitable sooner or later. What did those checks turn up on Thornaby?"

"Nothing, except he was on drugs squad until last year. He only came off because his three years were up. I do know he has a holiday home in Ireland, near Waterford."

"How on earth do you know that, Fred?"

"Coincidence, my wife and his wife are both in the WI. They went for a conference or something and she told me that Mrs Thornaby had been boasting about it."

"Interesting, I am just popping down to Personnel to find out who has been finding out our numbers. I think we will get them all changed after this is all over, do you want me to? How wise we were not to use them. Are things set up for tomorrow?"

"Yes, and I would like mine changed please. I think we all would. Everything is ready. Do you want any of us down at the college with you?"

"That is not a bad idea. One of you, maybe, I don't mind who, could stay in our offices at the college while the search is on. Mainly for security, and in case anything turns up. Who wants to do it? Any takers?"

Lauren laughed and said, "I've been told not to go near sheep while I am pregnant and I'm terrified of cows and I hate the countryside, I'd rather not."

"I am afraid I have an appointment with the medical officer here in the morning, I can reschedule it if you want?"

"No, Nita, I won't have you missing that. I know it is important and I think it might be to confirm you can come back to full duties again. That leaves you, Fred, would you mind?"

"Not at all, do you want me at the briefing?"

"I think not, can you go directly there?"

His visit to the personnel department was very interesting. He discovered that several attempts had been made to access information about the Operation Moon team by some rather unexpected officers. A couple of them made him feel very betrayed. He arrived back in the office with a sheaf of papers and handed them to Nita.

"Can you do checks on all these please, I am sorry it is a lot more work. Now, I suppose I had better hear what Thornaby has to say, down in my other office. I'll ring him."

Saul had to admit that Thornaby made a plausible explanation about believing Diana was wanted. The man lied so glibly that Saul developed a real dislike for him. He pretended to accept the story and even laughed off an attempt by Thornaby to ask about Diana's whereabouts. As Thornaby got up to leave, Saul said, "May I suggest that you concern yourself with your work, not mine? I do not appreciate officers nosing around in what does not concern them. You should know better. It is none of your business who was with me today. Should you ever get to my rank then you will know I have to do a lot of liaison with different agencies. You may well be aware the Operation Moon is concerned with currency fraud on a huge scale. That is why I had the visitors today."

Thornaby had the grace to blush.

"Sorry, sir. I'll get back to my division."

"I think that is an excellent idea."

The drugs raid on the college went very well. The search turned up far more than expected. Saul spoke with professor Hardaker after it was over.

"Things just get worse! I had no idea drugs were that much of a problem here! What did horrify me was the ones you found in the staff quarters. That Rachel, of all people should have them in her desk! Cannabis! Will she be prosecuted?"

"I doubt it, it was only a small amount for personal use I suspect. She will get a caution, and the offer of drug counselling."

"Thank you, I think I should tell you something. An academic friend of mine at Leeds University told me something yesterday, when I was at a seminar. He said that there was something strange going on here. He actually advised me to get out as soon as I can, before the wheel came off. When I pressed him he had been told by a policeman friend of his there was a big operation, and you were involved in it. Was it this raid?"

"I suppose it must have been, tell me who this man is."

Saul was very surprised when he found out who the police officer had been. He had known the man for years and would have thought he was both trustworthy and discreet. It was another name to add to the list. By the end of the week the covert search had been done at the college. The carelessness of the offenders had been stupid. He was talking to Celia about it.

"Did they really think because we had raided once, that was it? To use the same hiding places that we already knew about!

How stupid can you get? I think you have your promotion board next week? I have recommended you, very highly. The best of luck, Celia, I have been very impressed how you have taken on the Grady murder and the rest of what I have burdened you with. Even if they ask you what you are working on at the moment, you know you cannot say? Just tell them it is restricted information at the moment. ACC Kitchen is on your board I think, he will try to press you on it. This is what you tell him, learn it by heart and there should be no problems. The Chief will stop any of that line of questioning."

"Thank you, Saul. Mr Kitchen spoke to me last week and asked to see my desk diary. He was asking all sorts of questions and I told him just what you told us to. I was going to put him on the list but noticed he was already on it. I need to tell you something else, something personal. I have been seeing someone, not in the job, he is a company director of a big computer firm. His name is Andrew Rigby and he asked me to marry him, last week. I said yes. I shall continue in the force at least for a while, but I have prepared a report. Do I give it to you now, or after my board?"

"Oh, Celia, I am so pleased for you. At last, you have found someone. He is a lucky man. Give me the report and I will put it in after the board. It shouldn't make a difference but it might. Then I can say I knew about it. That is wonderful news and I felicitate you. You know when I got married I had to put in a report begging permission to marry! Thank goodness things have changed! When will the wedding be?"

"Probably in the autumn. I shall be most offended if you and Anna are not there. My father doesn't like Andrew, and says he will not come. My brother is too frightened of him to go against Father. I rather hoped you would give me away?"

"I would be flattered to. Why does your father disapprove?"

"Andrew is not an academic, he is a self-made man. He is quite a bit older than me. Father has got it into his head the marriage will not work."

"I expect he will come round. Do you want me to talk to him?"

"Would you? He likes you. He says you have a very good degree. I didn't know that."

"I got by. Leave it to me."

*

It was a day of surprises for Saul. When he got home his eldest son, Stephen, was there, with his girlfriend and their two dogs.

"This is a pleasant surprise, Stephen, to what do we owe the honour? Is your mother home yet? No, all right I'll put the kettle on. That looks like her car, yes it is."

"We want to tell you something, but Mum as well."

"If it is money you need you don't have to tell her. I can sort it out."

"No, it's not that."

Stephen would not be drawn. When Saul and Anna were in the kitchen he said, "Lissa and I have some news. She is expecting, and we have decided to get hitched. It is due in a few months, about five."

Anna burst into tears, which Saul almost expected. He liked Clarissa and smiled at her.

"Welcome to the family, Lissa. Son, you are a lucky chap! Congratulations, I trust all is well with mother and child?"

"So the doctors tell me, Mr Catchpole."

"Good, now it is Saul or Dad. I know I have other names, but they are not very nice. The latest one is Carrot Top which I haven't been called for years! Anna stop sniffling and pass me the corkscrew. This calls for something stronger. Come here, child, and give your father-in-law a kiss, I had better ring Sam and tell him."

"He already knows he is on his way over with Tatum."

There was something about the smug grin that alerted Saul. He said, "What are you not telling me?"

"Wait and see, Dad."

When Sam and Tatum announced their engagement about an hour later Saul began to laugh, Anna was silenced for at least five minutes before she was told it would not be a double wedding and then she wailed, "I'm going to be a grandmother!"

"Yes and don't tell me you haven't longed for it, because I know you have, you will be the youngest-looking Granny around. I think we will have to find a Glamorous Granny competition for you."

She threw a cushion at him, and he spilled champagne on his suit and had to go and change. Much later he realized Lysander had found and emptied his glass. He knew Anna would want a new outfit for each wedding and groaned. She had excellent taste, which was always expensive.

He rang his daughters at their boarding school and told them. They were thrilled they had been asked to be bridesmaids. Saul went and checked his bank balance. Things were going to be very expensive. He went to bed that evening a very happy and proud man.

Chapter Thirteen

The following evening, he had not long been back from work when he received a call. It was from Sandra Lancashire.

"I am so sorry to call so late, sir, but you did tell me to if anything worried me to ring you. Something odd has happened and I don't know what it means. I'd rather come and see you and don't want to talk here. Could I come and see you tomorrow?"

"No, I'll come and see you now. Where shall we meet up?"

"Do you know the Black Bull? I'll meet you in the lounge bar. Thanks, sir, I think it might be important."

Saul drove there straight away, and found her in the snug. He went and bought a drink for them, sat down and said, "Are you all right? It's all right, whatever it is you did the right thing. It is so gratifying when one of my officers actually listens to me and then does what I ask them to. Do you want to talk here or shall we go for a meal? I think there is a good Indian restaurant down the road."

"I think that might be better. You never know who is listening in this pub. They know me in here, and some of my colleagues come in here too."

At the restaurant they ordered a meal, and Sandra stretched for her purse, and Saul said, "No, I'll do this. Now what is worrying you?"

"I don't quite know what to do. It may be nothing but yesterday I went off duty, leaving my bag and all that in my locker, which I locked. I always double-check and the key is on my car keys so I know it is secure. This afternoon I came in very early, when I came on duty, the locker was locked, but when I opened it I knew someone had been inside it. They had very carefully searched everything. I was pretty cross but there was an urgent call, so I didn't have time to check everything carefully. I have just started a new pocket book, a few days ago. The old ones I keep in the locker under my old receipt books and kit belt and stab proof jacket. I got back to the station just before tea, and when I got to really search, I found the most recent pocket book and one before this one, is missing. With all the entries for the work I did on the squad. To say I was angry was an understatement. I went up to report it to Inspector Bradley but she has been off for a couple of days. I trust her and like her, I wasn't sure what to do, so while I was thinking about it, I took some crime complaints into the Detective Sergeant's office. He had been called down to the cell block, I think he was interviewing someone. I put the crime complaints in his in tray and then I noticed some numbers on a scrap of paper, and some jottings I don't understand. One of the numbers was your mobile one, and another was Karen Grady's mobile number, I know I shouldn't have but I picked it up and took a copy in the copying room next door and replaced it where I had found it. Here is the copy I took. Then as he wasn't back, I had a quick look round, and

I found photocopies of my missing pocket book in his waste bin, under some other stuff. I left them as I had found them. I had to go down and fill the car up with petrol, wrote the log book up and came back in, and had to take a statement up to his office and when I got there I noticed that the bit of paper had disappeared. I left the statement in his in tray. I got another call and had to go out to a job and when I got back and went to put things in my locker the missing pocket book was back, and the lock was once again locked. When I looked through the book I found several pages had disappeared, they have been very carefully cut out. That was worrying enough, but as you can see on that bit of paper is DG and a number of a mobile against it. Oh, yes mine is on there too."

"You have done the right thing. Is anything else missing from your locker?"

"Nothing very important, Karen gave me a photo of her and Eddie, I was going to return it to her, if she wanted it back. I also had a photo of me in there with my family and boyfriend. I know the photo of Karen and Eddie had gone but now it has been returned. Another thing is missing, in the back of the frame of my family photo, there was a letter from my sister, in its envelope. I had forgotten to take it home with me last week and was going to today. It has my address and hers on it."

"Is that it?"

"Well, no. That is all that is missing, yes but I decided to go back to my flat to ring you. I think someone has been in there as well. Things have been moved, not obviously and nothing important has gone. I was going to ring you on the land line but when I picked it up there was a very faint click so I went into the bathroom, put the shower on, and rang you on my mobile. I locked up and went straight to the Bull."

"What is the other thing that isn't important?"

"I think maybe I shouldn't have it. You know when we were looking at the scene of the murder, there were some things there. The scenes of crime dusted them checked them and recorded them and all that but amongst them was a ball point pen, one of those animal feed merchant ones, a Dectomax one. Dectomax is a sheep scab injectable a very good one and very common. They were going to chuck it but my pen was running out and they said I could have it."

"Yes they asked me if they could give it to you and I said yes, so stop fretting. Go on."

"Well, I took it more as a souvenir more than anything else. It stopped working within an hour or so, by which time I had found I had another one. I kept it anyway, because this is my first murder and I wanted to have it to remind me. I might never get on another squad. I kept it on my sideboard. That has gone. It was very heavy for a freebie, very heavy indeed. Do I report it?"

"You just have. Have you mislaid your keys recently?"

"Not mislaid, no. One of the lads on the shift borrowed them to get the backdoor open the other day, he had forgotten his, I asked him for them back when I remembered later that day. I don't know where he had dropped them because they smelled funny almost oily, rather sticky. Talking of smells, I know what that smell I couldn't identify was. It was dairy hypochlorite. It is a strong disinfectant used on farms, for cattle and sheep. My dad was using it on the farm the other day when I went back on my day off and I recognized it immediately."

"I can assure you this will not be your only turn on a murder squad, I want you to come on mine, as soon as you can. May I have permission to search your flat?"

"Of course you can, I warn you the bathroom is a bit untidy and I didn't wash up the breakfast things this morning. There are some dirty clothes under the sink. I was going to put them in the wash tonight."

"With two teenage daughters, I doubt that will worry me. I want you to go and stay with your parents for a few days. I will second you for a few days."

"I can't, I am in court tomorrow with a drink-driver and a shoplifter."

"Go from your parents. Someone will pick you up and stay with you all day. Then they will take you home and stay with you after that. What was the job you got sent to when you first came on duty?"

"Yes that was a bit odd. It was reported as an accident right at the far end of our patch, up a country lane. When I got there, no trace. There are dry stone walls either side of the road and there was no sign of damage. I found someone drystone walling not far away, he said not only had there not been an accident there, mine was the only vehicle he had seen in the lane all day."

"This came from control room?"

"Yes it was an anonymous male caller."

"Ok, Sandra, thank you, you have done it exactly right. I will come back with you to get whatever you need from your flat. Do you have to go back to the station? No, you have the correct pocket book? You have your uniform?"

"I have all my pocket books with me, sir. I thought you had all our pocket books copied before we left the squad didn't you? Here is the one with the pages taken out of it."

"Yes, whoever is behind this doesn't know that, it would seem, which means they have never been on my squad. I always do it, just so I don't have to track something down later. Take the keys you need off the key ring and give me the others."

Together they went to her flat and she got everything she needed. Before she drove off Saul checked her car and after she had gone he called in a team, who dusted for fingerprints, and found the bug that had been put into her phone, and removed it. He called an emergency locksmith and had the door locks changed.

His next stop was at her police station, where he went into the CID office together with several of the murder squad, and found the detective Sergeant sitting at his desk.

"Good evening, Bernie, I am so glad I have found you, look we need to do a raid this evening, very much at the last minute and if we wait, the evidence may be moved. We have had an anonymous tip-off and I have managed to get hold of a magistrate but half my officers are committed on something else and I need help. Would you oblige? I need a Skipper to supervise. It isn't far away and I am waiting for some more troops to arrive. It is all hands on deck on it. Could you take care of the documentation for me?"

"Of course, sir, be pleased to. Where is it?"

"Here I'll write it down, where I want everyone to meet up, oh, I think my pen is running out, I'll use this one."

He picked up a Dectomax biro from the desk and sat down at a nearby table.

"Not that one, sir, it doesn't work either, I'll find you another."

"No problem, it seems to have worked but is obviously on its last legs, I'll put it in the bin on my way downstairs."

Saul put it in his suit jacket pocket.

"Here get hold of what you need and meet me here. I must just ring control room and I will meet you there. Can you take these two officers in your vehicle?"

Saul went out to his vehicle parked just down from the police station, and handed the pen to Geoff Bickerstaff, who was waiting for him, and said, "Did you manage to get one? Yes, it looks identical, great! This one is much heavier than yours, there has got to be something special about it. Get it to the lab as soon as you can, I believe it is some sort of explosive's fuse so treat it gently. If he asks for it I will give him this one, he can hardly say there is anything special about this one, without letting the cat out of the bag. I also picked this up from the desk when he wasn't looking. There are some things written on there that shouldn't be, like my home address for a start. Find out what you can about everything on there, like whose numbers they are. The other two are watching him. I'll bet he phones someone, the raid is on someone I know is a crony of his, at a pub."

"Sorry, guv, where is your address?"

"The house number and post code. My landline number, which is not that surprising as it is in control room for when they need to call me out, and everyone has my mobile number. There is also my car registration number here which I do find very odd. Let me know. I will keep you in touch. As soon as we leave, Lorraine Bradley will come and liaise with you. When I spoke to her she confided in me that she has had her suspicions about Bernie Rush for a while."

"Celia is going to ask to borrow Bernie's phone, when she drops hers and breaks it. She is ready to download everything on his phone before she gives it back. It is all fixed, tell me, is this really a raid, I mean was there one planned?"

"Yes it is a real one and no it wasn't planned and I doubt we will find much. If I am not mistaken, is Thornaby the one in charge for this sub-division?"

"You very seldom are, sir, and yes he covers this station from the next one over. May I make a personal comment, sir?"

"Of course you may, Geoff."

"I never did like him or Bernie Rush much. You do know they are related don't you?"

"No I didn't, in what way?"

"I believe they are half-brothers."

"Now how on earth did you find that out?"

"It was a long time ago, when Bernie and I were playing a rugby match together. He was quite a useful fly half in his time. We had won, I think against Nottingham force. We all went and got rat-arsed in the police club that evening. We were both in uniform then, and I was just due to start on CID. Bernie told me he would be joining me soon and when I asked how he knew and he told me Thornaby was his half-brother and that he was certain to get it. If you look at them, they are not unlike, except Rush is balding and Thornaby is grey and a bit fatter."

"I see what you mean, now I come to think about it. What else do you know about them?"

"Not much, I'll write it down for you. You had better get going."

The raid was not quite as unproductive as they had anticipated. Although it was obvious that the pub landlord had received a tip-off, heard by two officers already in the bar under cover, he had not had time to empty the garage, and a quantity of high value stolen goods were found, including several wide screen televisions and computers and a firearm. One of Saul's team had taken on the investigation. At the debrief, Rush had seemed as shocked as anyone, but after he left, the two officers who had been with him told Saul he had gone into the gents and made a phone call just before they left for the pub. Celia had successfully managed to download the phone's recent activity and the call was confirmed as coming from Rush's phone. Saul immediately reported the details to the Chief Constable who was aware of the raid and its intentions and had authorized it. Before the debrief was over Rush had asked Saul for the pen back with a rather pathetic excuse that he had borrowed the pen from a friend, for whom it had sentimental attachment. Saul had handed the duplicate one over and said, "I think I managed to get it to work, sorry about that, with all this going on I quite forgot."

What Rush did not know was that the pen he had been handed back had a locator chip inserted into the plastic of it and the pen's movements were being recorded. This was also authorised by the Chief. When Saul finally got home it was way after three a.m. He was very glad to get to bed.

Chapter Fourteen

Saul watched as Diana walked down the country lane towards him with Drift at her side. Drift was delighted to see him and wagged her tail enthusiastically when they met. They moved over to a huge boulder by the road and sat down.

"How are you feeling, Di, are you healed?"

"Much better thanks. Look, things are getting terribly imminent, but you know that. You know the plans for the day after tomorrow? You have to get me and Nick away. One of the VIPs knows me as someone else, and he knows me rather too well. Another knows Nick. If they see either of us before it all goes down, it might just get called off for later time when we are not prepared. It is all set up."

"Are you looking for this pen, Di?"

"Yes, frantically, we have been for ages, I know you said you had it and it would get to us, but I need it. I need to put it somewhere so someone can use it or try to. Do you know its secret?"

"Yes, it was a fuse that will set everything off. It isn't any more it has been altered. Your chaps asked me to give it to you today. I replaced it with another one which is at the moment up at the college just here on this plan."

"Let me guess, in Ruth's locker?

"You got it in one. I believe in her jacket pocket. How will you swap it? You have not been contacted on your phone for a few days. You need to change it. Your number, I discovered is known to some people who shouldn't have it. I have here a new one, again, given by your chaps. You need to use this from now on."

"Oh bother, I shall have to re-programme it, it will take a while. Swapping it won't be a problem. I will do it at coffee time. She always hangs hers on a hook outside the canteen and often I hang mine next to it. You see, although Ruth knows that someone is suspected of being an infiltrator she doesn't know it is me. She thinks their traitor is Alison."

"I should have spotted or my officers should, that your phone is far too heavy and a little too large and rather unusual. Do I need to do anything about the docks at Tilbury?"

"No, that is already being covered by us. I knew you would pick up on that, you clever dog!"

"I have something to tell you. I have to change my phone too, I am working with your lot, or will be in the future, under cover in the job I do now but now I have another agenda. I had no idea how badly we had been infiltrated. It will take years to find out everybody. Right, tell me how I get you into custody. You and Nick."

"It doesn't have to be you."

"Oh believe me, it does!"

"I must be taken to where no one will recognize me, from the lot arriving with all the VIPs. Nick too."

"Don't worry. That is all covered, what do we do with the dogs?"

"They will have to come too, be careful if you lay hands on either of us you may get bitten, I suggest you wear body armour. Drift has excellent teeth."

"Noted. I must go now, we will be in the sheep unit by six in the morning, and I will come there about half seven. We will, of course, search the whole place the day before, as we would for any high-profile visit of royalty and heads of states, and our PM. I take it they intend to put the bombs there after that?"

"I hope so because I will be defusing it as soon as they have left. Me and a couple of others, who no one suspects because they have very much blended in here and have been here a while. I know who they are but no one else does."

"Because you are actually the officer in charge of all this, I think."

"You think too much. No comment."

"Which is why I've been recruited."

"Possibly. Now mean it when you arrest me. I will, I promise give you just cause!"

"That's what worries me! Take care of yourself and Anna sends her love."

"And mine to both of you, and of course, Hector and Lysander!"

*

The briefing of all the officers on duty at the royal visit and the visit of so many heads of state and politicians took place at five thirty in the morning at the Assembly Hall of the college. There were several hundred officers from all sorts of departments. After it was done, they began to disperse and the officers on stand-by were sent down to the sheep unit, which although it was to be visited by the dignitaries was not the principal theatre of their attention. By seven thirty they were waiting in the main sheep shed, where teas and coffees had been laid on and they were able to use the toilet facilities nearby. Almost every senior officer from the local force was needed to provide sufficient cover and Saul Catchpole had been designated to ensure that all those at the sheep unit were ready in case they were needed. He was standing just outside the main building when a heated argument was heard from the sheep pens next door. The volume increased as Saul with several other officers arrived. The argument appeared to be about the death of a lamb.

"And I'm telling you I did not over feed it! I tubed it exactly as I should have done, I told you it didn't need feeding, I thought it had already been fed, its tummy seemed taut, but you insisted. It's not down to me. Ask which one of the others fed it, I bet someone did. You are only upset because it's one of your stupid lumbering Suffolks. You and Suffolks seem to have a lot in common. Your trouble is you just don't listen to any of us. Here, take it, do an autopsy, I think it is watery mouth."

"You stupid, arrogant bitch, I've been a shepherd for years and it is not your place to tell me. What would you know? Give it here then we will soon solve this, we will cut it open and I'll prove you wrong."

They were attracting quite an audience. Alison moved in but backed off when Diana almost flung the lamb at Nick. It hit him soundly in the face and he staggered back with blood pouring from his mouth. Saul wondered if he had really lost his temper when he hit Diana back, and a real physical scrap began between the two of them. Saul could hear the thumps of real hard blows. He stepped in, grabbed hold of Diana and said in a very authoritative tone, "Stop it now the pair of you! You, hold her, you grab him, for God's sake keep hold of him!"

The lamb came flying back and hit Saul in the chest, almost knocking him over. It was at this point he realized just how much a large lamb can weigh. It was very heavy and he stepped back at which point Nick broke free of the officer restraining him and lunged at Diana who twisted neatly out of the grip of the woman officer. She and Nick exchanged more blows. The language from the pair of them made Saul wince.

"Right the pair of you are under arrest. Grab them and get them both in the van, in separate cages. Let their dogs in with them or we will all get bitten. They can cool off in there, but I am not having the visitors subjected to this kind of disgraceful behaviour so I had better go and explain the reasons for the arrest to the custody officer at the station, I will be back before everything kicks off."

He followed the custody van for a couple of miles down the road and out of sight. The van pulled into the driveway of a large and apparently unoccupied house and stopped and Callum Doyle, the driver, got out and opened the front door with a key. Saul pulled up beside him. Callum said, "That was pretty impressive, sir, it looked very real to me. Are you all right? That lamb hit you with quite a thump!"

"I will probably live. You know what to do? I rather enjoyed that! Come on we had better let them out and it looks like a little first aid might be in order."

In the house in a room at the back of the building that could not be seen from outside, there were furnishings. Diana and Nick giggling rather childishly, and four dogs were settled in there and Callum said, "Let's have a look at that cut lip of yours, Mr Greenwood."

"It isn't cut, that was just a theatrical blood capsule. I'm not hurt. Thanks though."

Saul looked with resignation at Diana.

"I suppose you are fine too? You were going at it hammer and tongs, it sounded real enough."

"I know, we are both all right, we were only play acting. Good, now we can get some kip, we have only been up for about thirty-six hours. For your information we replaced all the explosives with dummy stuff, except for the one lot. Your lads will be in no danger; the bomb disposal lot know where to go. The fuse will have blown up the foyer part of the building, that I understand the college was going to have demolished anyway as it was deemed unsafe, and they have plans for a new one. That way the offenders can be charged with using explosives with intent to endanger life. Of course, as the foyer was condemned the VIPs will not be using it, and will go in through another entrance. The published plan said they would, though."

"Yes, that was what was emphasised at the briefing earlier."

Callum said, "So some of our lot are at least suspected, I gather."

"Most definitely, Callum. There are quite a few in this force alone who are involved and we need to catch them. This has been planned for long time, to assassinate the Irish Prime minister, the Taoiseach, and take a few others with him, and one of our royal family too. It would be a terrific coup to get so many for this terrorist organization. Hopefully it will go as we have engineered. One of the ministers from Ireland is involved and wants and hopes to take over, I suspect he will detach himself from the main group on some excuses, so he does not come to harm. He is being monitored very closely."

"Sir, didn't they try this once before, a couple of years ago, at a place down in Surrey, again agricultural, some sort of Orchid place?"

"That was foiled too, but the main instigator escaped and went off on some sort of plant hunt in Thailand I think it was. He was convicted but they never got the main man behind it who had been very careful to keep himself detached. I must get back, you look after these two reprobates. I warn you they will run rings round you given the slightest opportunity! Behave yourself you two!"

Saul returned after a suitable amount of time to the sheep shed. What was not obvious to a few officers that were not from his force was that all the officers on standby seemed to know each other, and were not relaxing and were waiting as if poised for action. One of the Inspectors from a visiting force came to Saul and said, "Is something about to happen?"

"Oh yes, how very astute of you. What I want you and your officers to do is to remain here and secure this building and not let anyone in, unless they comply with these written orders. Here, read these written orders from your Chief Constable. I would have given them to you in about ten minutes. In a little while you will hear an explosion. Don't panic, it won't hurt anyone. We need it to expose someone. Your chief has hand-picked all of you for this, because of your abilities. This is to be the safe house for the dignitaries that will be brought to you."

He handed several other envelopes to other officers and then called all the supervisors together and asked if there were any problems with their orders. He emphasised that no officer was to leave the sheep shed area until he gave the order and all mobile phones had to be handed in and switched off until the end of the operation. Once everything was made clear, they waited, and a little while later there was the sound of a huge explosion from the main building about a quarter of a mile away. Saul nodded and the police teams that had formed up ready to go sprang into action.

The bomb disposal arrived within minutes and the dignitaries were safely taken away and the mop-up operation started. It went very smoothly and numerous arrests were made and the suspects were taken away. One officer, whom Saul knew and had trusted, and who had tried to sneak out of the sheep shed area with his mobile phone just after the orders had been disclosed, was also arrested. As he was being put into the prison van he shouted at Saul, "You bastard! To think I put up with you for two years and you knew about this, all along!"

Saul who felt very betrayed and not a little angry retorted,

"It may comfort you to know, when you have time to reflect in your prison cell, that I didn't know. I am just glad that I got some decent work out of you before you elected to become a turn coat, or were you always a traitor?"

The officer spat at Saul as the doors of the van were closed.

Saul knew he had only been part of an enormous operation that had been painstakingly contrived. His job now was to ensure that all the criminals and terrorists involved and their helpers were exposed and convicted. The evidence, collected over two years or more was overwhelming, the main conspirator's visit to England had provided the security forces with an opportunity to ensure he was unable to claim diplomatic immunity from prosecution. The Taoiseach had been only too delighted when the plot had been disclosed to him to withdraw any such immunity from his aspiring assassin. That the dignitaries who had been saved were grateful was demonstrated by numerous awards made to officers from the security forces.

It took weeks to track everyone down and Saul made a point of being with the arresting officers when Thornaby and Rush were detained. Their expressions when they saw him there were a source of infinite pleasure to him and confirmed his belief in a God. He also knew that much of the evidence had been unearthed and supplied by Diana, and to a lesser extent Nick, but her name was not mentioned. He realized that she must have worked up to twenty hours a day at times. He saw almost nothing of her after the main event. She had returned to the college as the student she was and obtained a distinction at the end of her course.

Professor Hardaker invited him to the presentation at the end of the course, but Diana was not there. After, he was invited to drinks with the staff. He went for a wander around the buildings. In the main reception, there were many photographs of courses that had been run at the college. He found the one of her sheep course but neither she or Nick were mentioned, nor were there any photographs of them. In the car park by the residential block he found her with Drift loading up her car. He went over to her.

"No photograph of you in the gallery? I wonder why?"

"I'm not photogenic. I wanted to see you to say goodbye and thank you for all you have done, both for me personally and my department. Do you want to meet up for a drink somewhere?"

"If you like, but why not come to our place for a couple of days? Anna keeps saying she wants to see you again."

"I wish I could but my job here is done and another one is about to start. Where shall we meet?"

"The Angel, at Hetton? I'll treat you."

"That would be wonderful, when?"

"Tomorrow, seven? I'll book a table."

"Thank you, I'll be there."

*

Saul arrived at the pub rather early and waited for her to arrive. He watched the car park filling up and noticed a Lamborghini pull up and thought that it was not that unusual a place to see such a car as the clientele were rather wealthy and the food was renowned. He was wondering if she would be on time, when the stunning red head who had been driving the Lamborghini, said from beside him, "Are you expecting someone else, Saul?"

He looked at her, dumbstruck. The transformation was complete and she could have been a movie star, her outfit was from a top fashion house, her make up perfect and she looked totally glamorous. She smiled and said, "One day you might see the real me. I think it is more what you know than what you see now."

He pulled himself together and noticed the admiring and rather envious glances he was getting from several men in the bar area.

"What can I get you to drink?"

"I'd like a pint of Boddingtons, please. I like a good northern pint from time to time."

It was so out of character that he wondered about her request but did not argue. They went and sat in a quiet corner of the restaurant. He said, "Diana, I want to ask you something. If ever you need refuge or assistance at any time, or just somewhere to go or hide or somewhere to stay, will you come to me and Anna? All you have to do is turn up, or ring and I will come and get you, wherever you are. We both admire you immensely you know. I think everyone needs a safe haven from time to time and I hope we can offer you that. I owe you that at least. Anna is desperate for you to come to us for Christmas."

Diana smiled and said, "That is the nicest thing you could have said, and I love you both for it. Yes, I will if I can, I count you as true friends. Now, what do you want to know?"

"As much as you can tell me. I am very curious."

"Insatiably I should say. All right. Nick was put into the college three years ago, as we knew it was being considered as a location for something. When Mike was appointed as Sheep Tutor we knew we were on the right track. He was not exactly unknown to us. We knew that they intended to get the world's attention and that they wanted to kill as many well-known dignitaries as they could. It is all to do with their warped idea of freedom. I was therefore enrolled as a student and watched and waited. I think I knew Eddie was in some way connected to Mike from the beginning. Had you noticed any similarities about them?"

"Both much the same build, fair hair, blue eyes, fresh complexion."

"They also had hardly any ear lobes and both of them had club feet. Eddie only the one but I noticed one day when we all got soaked and Mike took his shoes and socks off and I saw his feet that both his were slightly deformed. I was able to work out from a pretty early stage that Eddie was unhinged. Mike was just nasty. I made a point of knowing who he spoke to or was friendly with and who rather pointedly avoided him or a close association with him. The marks fiasco was just Mike's hatred of women, combined with a sense of power and his own importance. He did not want women to excel in what he considered a man's world. One of my briefs was to hinder him and make life as difficult as I could without blowing my cover, I rather enjoyed that and did my best! The lamb looks nice."

"I've gone off lamb recently. Please tell me you didn't kill that lamb for my benefit?"

"Off course not. It had died a couple of weeks before and had been put in the freezer for autopsy later, and we used it. It was the largest one I could find. Your expression was splendid when it hit you. I shall live off that for some years!"

"If I could have spanked you then and there I would have done. I think I will have the mushroom risotto. Go on."

"I might have enjoyed that! I'll have the beef please. At the beginning of the course it was obvious Eddie knew Steve.

Alison was just a bit too pally with Eddie, considering what a shit he was. Alison was often in odd places at odd times. I believe she was the coordinator, and knew who was what. I suspect they didn't know each other unless they had to. I found the hiding place in the culvert very early. They had a post box there, and I think I got all of the messages, bar maybe the first one. When I wasn't there Nick substituted for me. I found out who was leaving the messages, your DCI Thornaby chap. I once saw someone who looked a bit like him but a bit balder and a bit thinner put something in there, but it was written by Thornaby, I recognized the handwriting. Things were coming together very well until Eddie started to lose the plot. First of all, with Zoe, then with anyone else who upset him. That he has serious mental problems is obvious. As well as being plain bad!

He didn't give a fig about the course and did no work on it. I am so glad that Janet has got and is looking after his dog now. Mike needed him and was desperate to keep him on the course. When Eddie got together with Billy's daughter, for the purpose of pushing drugs to feed his cocaine habit, he was careless. Billy got very suspicious and spoke to Thornaby about it, who in turn told Mike who in turn told Eddie. I saw Thornaby and Mike together one evening. Mike didn't live that far from college and my walks often took me out that way."

"In other words you were watching him."

"Of course I was. Eddie then must have decided that the easiest thing was to get rid of Billy, so he faked the suicide. We panicked a bit then. We knew Eddie was hiding a large stash of drugs and explosives at a place called Ghyll House, there is a cave up near there. I think, but am not sure, that Billy was killed either on the way to it or having found it and on the way back to call the police. We moved the body and believe me if we could have stopped the murder we would have done but we were too late. Ah, here is your meal."

They waited until the meal was served and then she continued, "McGill took an instant dislike to Eddie. He thought him less than useless and said so. Then he caught him hiding something. I am not sure what but he kicked him off the farm there and then. And reported him to Mike but I think he was a bit doubtful about Mike and said he was going to the police. It was about then Eddie lost control. I do know that McGill had made some sort of comment about Eddie being a warped and unpleasant cripple. Eddie went back to fetch wages he was owed and killed him. We didn't want Thornaby investigating so we moved him to the railway line, out of Thornaby's jurisdiction."

"There must have been more than the two of you watching all this."

"Yes there must. Eddie decided to hit on Karen Grady. He had often been to Grady's house and when he wanted to be was fun. The poor kid fell for it. Mike saw the danger signals and decided that Eddie needed replacing. Eddie knew this was a strong possibility by this time. I am sure you had the report on the explosives. The plan was to put them all in a sequence so that after the first one, everyone would seek shelter in another building which in turn would blow up and so on. It was to be set off by a powerful fuse that would begin the sequence. Ruth was the explosives expert. Alison was the communicator, Mike was the facilitator and Eddie was to move and hide the explosives until they were required. He was their pack horse you might say and I think, had he survived, they would have disposed of him after it was over or even at the time. The fuse was made abroad with some very specialized knowledge and brought into the country just before Mike was murdered."

"Steve, his supposed funeral in France?"

"That's right, his aunt, whose name incidentally he couldn't remember!"

"How did he get it through customs?"

"He went by ferry as a foot passenger, and he put it in his specs case, which incidentally is lead lined. He gave it to Mike, because they no longer trusted Eddie. Their other explosives came in through Tilbury where several arrests have been made. Eddie knew it had been delivered, and had a huge row with Mike, so I am told, and Eddie was told he was leaving. Eddie suggested a farewell drink, drugged Mike and then decided he hated him that much that the plot was no longer important to him and decided to have a bit of sadistic fun with him before finally killing him. It was as much Mike's refusal to accept him as a full son, rather than an illegitimate mistake that caused such hatred. What he didn't know, and neither did we, was what the fuse looked like. All the time he had Mike in his power he had the fuse but didn't know it. He realized he needed an alibi for Mike's death so set up the rope trick, so Mike must have had a horrific death."

"If he had found and identified the fuse what good would it have done him?"

"They would have had to keep him around. They needed him again."

"Oh, I see."

"Nick missed Mike. And wondered where he had gone with Eddie. Then he missed the tractor. He couldn't search everywhere so when he saw Eddie a bit later he very discreetly followed him, which of course he had been trained to do. Eddie had gone back to gloat and was laughing as he came away. As soon as Eddie had gone, Nick checked but Mike was well and truly dead, so Nick moved the body to the railway line. He was going to hide him in the culvert, but he heard the train coming and hid in there himself until the train went again. He got away the other side of the line. It was him I think your passengers saw. Then the unexpected happened. Eddie went back, couldn't find the body but did see the train stop and obviously the driver had found something, so he waited and then went over to check, just before your WPC arrived with the college security man. He too hid in the culvert, hence he knew what she looked like and her name. He slunk off soon afterwards."

"I think in future that anyone attending a body should have another officer with them. He could have killed my officer."

"Yes he could. Then we discovered what the fuse looked like. We spent hours trying to find it. Nick searched as did others. We even got your crime property cupboard checked but then one of Thornaby's officers remembered seeing Sandra Lancashire with one like it."

"The one who tried to slip away on the day and warn the others that things were not what they thought and it was a trap?"

"That is the one. She had been on your squad so was obviously suspect to them. You all were, and because you had dealings with me, I became a person of interest to them. They were not sure who I was, and thought I needed investigating. Hence the fictitious warrant. It was Thornaby's intention to question me and find out. They needed to know what I knew. I swapped the pens in Ruth's coat pocket, and the one you had given her provided us with good evidence as to where she went, who she met and has been most helpful. I do thank you for arranging the inspection of all those explosive stores at mines and quarries. That let us know where a lot of things were moved to. This is a lovely meal, thank you so much."

"Diana, if that is even your name, am I ever going to see you again?"

"I have been promised this is the last big job. I hope so."

"Why do you do it? You told Anna it was a sort of patriotism but you must get something out of it. What do they give you at the end of it?"

"There are some peers who get honoured at about retirement time."

"Will you get that?"

"I don't need it. They can't really promote me, so I just do it, as I told you before, because I can."

They finished their meal with amicable small talk, and she drove off in the Lamborghini. He drove home in his Saab.

Chapter Fifteen

It was months later, after Saul had finished his part in Operation Moon, and he had been busy with other cases, that he was just coming back to his office when the Headquarters receptionist called to him as he entered the main door.

"Sir, there are two gentlemen waiting to see you, I've sat them over in the waiting area. They produced a Home Office identification to me."

Saul approached the men and said, "Mr Smith, Mr Jones, how may I help you, shall we go to a private office to talk?"

They declined an offer of refreshment and confirmed they were working with Diana. One of them said, "We know you can be discreet. She asked for you to have this. We are sorry. Don't read it in company, and take the case with you."

They left Saul a little bewildered. He decided to go home and read the letter there. No one was in when he got back and he sat with Hector and Lysander in the conservatory.

With the letter, was a key, which he put aside with the case.

Dear Saul,

Before soldiers go into battle, they prepare for the worst. That is what I am doing now. Putting my house in order.

The fact that you have been given this means one of two things. I am either dead, or missing, presumed dead. Either way, Diana Green will not be coming back. They promised me this would be the last job, before I retire. It will be the most important one and the biggest one yet.

When I told you I had no family, it was true. In some ways it is a requirement of the job. It makes it lonely, but there are compensations. Knowing there is no grieving family helps. You and Anna gave me friendship and respite. I have seldom been as happy and relaxed as I was when I stayed with you. I thought it right to tell you that you can no longer expect me to come at Christmas. I wish you all the best.

I have left my farm and Drift to Janet, in the knowledge that it will be the best for both of them. I have settled enough money on her to set her up on the farm and the life she deserves. She was a good friend to me and I always wished I could have been more honest with her.

There will be no funeral or memorial, that is the way it has to be. In the case you will find some things that it is inappropriate for Janet to keep. I have included a couple of bottles of wine in the hopes you and Anna will quietly drink a toast to our friendship.

Do not mourn the death of Diana Green. She never really existed. Sometime, when you are indulging in a good northern pint, remember me. I am sure you will work it out. My love to you and Anna, I am sure you will break it to her gently. I just felt you had a right to know.

Diana Green

Saul felt a lump in his throat and opened the case to find two bottles of incredibly expensive wine and some crystal goblets, one engraved with a picture of Diana the goddess of hunting and the other one with Diana the goddess of the moon. He put them in his display cabinet. In the case was a box in which were a lot of medals, including the George Cross and a bar to it. There was no name but there were dates. He went and found the photograph he had never given back to her, and put it with the goblets in the cabinet.

By the time Anna got home he was drunk. He chose his words to his wife very carefully and they both remained in shock for some time. He often looked at the orchid in the conservatory and each time he sniffed the scent he remembered her.

*

It took some time to track down Janet. He found her on a pleasant well-kept farm. As he drove up the drive to the farmhouse he saw Janet bringing in a flock of sheep to the farm yard. Drift and two other dogs were working with her. He waited patiently until the sheep were secured and Janet came over to him. Drift wagged her tail at him. Janet stared at him, frowned and said, "You are that detective. The one from the college. Why are you here?"

"I wanted to talk to you, I see you have Diana's dog, Drift with you."

"Yes she was left to me with the farm. I am only too pleased to give her a loving home. She is all that I have of Diana. She was a good friend to me you know. I am convinced she saved my life a couple of times. She was a very brave woman, look what she did for Zoe. When the solicitor told me she had left me all this I was stunned, and very distressed to hear of her death. He told me the funeral had taken place and the ashes had been scattered. Do you want to talk about her?"

"Yes please."

"Come in, and I'll make a brew."

They sat at the kitchen table, and she said, "What did you want to see me about?"

"I wanted to make sure you were all right and Drift had come to you. Now I know that things have turned out as Diana wanted, I have found out what I needed."

"Yes Drift has settled down well, and so has Eddie's dog. Did you go to Diana's funeral?"

"No I didn't know until afterwards either. Did you hear that Eddie has been detained during Her Majesty's Pleasure, which means he is insane and will never get out of detention, he is in Rampton hospital for the criminally insane."

"Good. That is where he needs to be. Can I ask you something?"

"I am not sure I'll know the answer but yes."

"She was a lot more than a student wasn't she? After that terrorist thing, I knew someone had to be working on the inside. I think it was her. I think you know."

"Yes. I do. All I can tell you is that she was the most courageous woman I have ever met. By taking her dog on you have done for her the thing she wanted most. Thank you. She thought a lot of you and I know she wanted you to be happy here. Are you?"

"Yes very. Because there is no grave to visit, I have done something else. There is a beautiful little valley here with a small waterfall and a pool. I go there to sit and think. I have called it Hunter's Peace. You know, after Diana, goddess of hunting. She did leave me something else, it was a photo of her and me together. I think Amy took it. On the back Diana had written 'A person dies twice, once when their body stops working and the next time is when the last person who remembers them dies. I hope I shall be around for a while!'"

*

The squad and all the officers who had worked on Operation Cain and Operation Moon were called in to headquarters to attend a debrief. The Chief Constable thanked all of them for their work and dedication and several announcements were made. Celia had been promoted and was leaving the squad. Others were moving on, and general observations were requested about how things could have been done better. Then Saul addressed the meeting and thanked them all and said, "I just have one more thing to say, and David and Geoff and Sandra might be especially interested. We have finally found out Eddie Sullivan's true identity. He used a number of aliases but the birth certificate gives his name as Cain Seth Wooler. David had it right all the time!

*

Stephen was married to Clarissa in Sevenoaks in Kent where she had been brought up. The ceremony went well and the whole family enjoyed it. Anna was tearful and Saul decided to cheer her up before they returned to Yorkshire.

He found a rather exclusive florists and went inside. There was an interesting selection of orchids inside. He had thought about Diana and her letter many times and it niggled him. It was almost as if she has included a message in it but he hadn't worked it out. Always when she had said he would work it out she had meant him to solve a clue. He and Anna had begun to collect a few orchids, it rather comforted them. In the shop he spotted a quite rare one, and asked the florist where it had come from.

He found the orchid centre just outside Tunbridge Wells. He pulled in and parked his car in the car park and went inside and looked around. There was a woman planting up at the back of the hot house, and as he walked towards her a young man, apparently the manager, came hurrying after him.

"Can I help you? I'm sorry, I was on the phone. Are you interested in any particular orchid?"

Saul replied, "Yes, several, but I am trying to find the black orchid. I have just started to grow some and that is one I would like."

As he spoke the woman at the back of the hot house looked up. For a moment there was a look of surprise on her face before she turned and walked out through a back entrance. By the time Saul got there she had disappeared. The young man rushed after him and said, "Sir, that is private, whatever is the matter? We don't have the black orchid at the moment but could get one for you. That lady could not help you, she is deaf and dumb, but a good worker."

"I am sorry. I thought I saw someone I knew for a moment, but I was obviously mistaken. Can I have your card and I will get back to you? I'll leave it for now thanks."

Suddenly he needed fresh air. By the time he got outside his head was spinning. He needed to sit down and found an ornamental bench. It took him a while before he felt well enough to drive. He walked to his car, unlocked it and got in. He sat in the driver's seat and stared out of the window. Then he noticed a small envelope on the dash board, and had no idea how it could have got there. He opened it up and read the brief message.

Well done you worked it out! Are we still on for Christmas?

At the bottom of the paper was a small sketch of a sheep and under it was written, *1 hoot 4 yes, 2 4 no.*

He looked around but the only person in sight was the manager returning into the building. Once the man was inside, Saul started the car and drove slowly from the car park hooting the horn just once at a passing cat. He distinctly heard a single chime of a bell. It was a very still day with no wind.